LONE STAR CHRISTMAS MISSION NOVELLA

Delores Fossen

Lone Star Books

Copyright © 2024 Delores Fossen

All rights reserved

The characters and events portrayed in this book are fictitious. Any similarity to real persons, living or dead, is coincidental and not intended by the author.

No part of this book may be reproduced, or stored in a retrieval system, or transmitted in any form or by any means, electronic, mechanical, photocopying, recording, or otherwise, without express written permission of the publisher.

ISBN-13: 9781965032084

Library of Congress Control Number: 2018675309
Printed in the United States of America

To Finley, Luke and Ruth

CHAPTER ONE

———— ★☆★ ————

Cash Whitaker silently cursed when he stepped into the house and saw the blood. Blood that was nearly the same color as the shattered red Christmas ornaments next to it.

Don't let it be her blood. Don't let it be Kayla's.

Those were the thoughts, the prayers, and the pleas that were pulsing in his head. The fear was ripping through him the same way that someone had torn through this living room.

With his Glock in a death grip in his hand, Cash kept moving, kept listening. Kept watching for a kidnapper, or a possible killer, as he threaded his way through the carnage.

The sofa and chairs had long, jagged cuts in them, exposing the fluffy white filling that looked like snow. What was left of the Christmas tree lay smashed and battered on the hardwood floor. The wrapped presents around it had been stomped on, the ribbons and contents crushed.

With the exception of the overhead light, every

possible glass object and bit of decor in the room had been broken. The mirror above the fireplace. The windows and lamps. The Santa and angel figurines that he guessed had once been on the mantel and end tables.

Had the kidnapper left the overhead light intact so Cash would have no trouble seeing that blood and the destruction?

Maybe.

The mess could have been designed to be a distraction. And it was. But setting up a distraction was far better than an out of control rage from some strung-out asshole who might have taken Kayla.

Cash saw more blood, splattered drops of it that led out of the living room and toward the hall. Cash followed the grisly trail, still listening for any signs of life.

There weren't any.

But he refused to believe she could be dead. No, Kayla had to be alive. He'd already failed her once. A big assed failure that had crushed her soul. And his. He couldn't fail her again.

"I've got the money," he lied, calling out to…well, whoever the hell had sent him the text.

Come alone. No cops. No Maverick Ops buddies. Bring 50K to 614 Shelter Lane by midnight or Kayla Morgan dies.

The text had arrived at 11:30 pm. Definitely not enough time for him to gather a ransom demand and get here before that deadline. And Cash had a bad feeling that the money hadn't been a strong motive in the kidnapper getting him to come here. No, this felt like more.

Like a sick kind of déjà vu.

Cash had thankfully been familiar with both the rural address outside of San Antonio and the home owner, Kayla Morgan. Yes, he knew her, and he couldn't let her die. That's why he'd started the half hour drive straight here from his house in the Texas Hill Country to a rural area just outside of San Antonio. Along the way, he'd also called his boss, Ruby Maverick, head of an elite security force, Maverick Ops.

Of course, Ruby had insisted he wait for backup, and as one of her operatives, Cash would have normally followed her orders to a tee.

Well, to a tee-ish anyway.

Sometimes, criminals and therefore the missions couldn't play by the rules or have the luxury of backup. It was already three minutes until midnight, and if he waited, it'd be way too late.

He'd done plenty of dangerous solo missions before. First in military special forces and for the last five years, missions for Maverick Ops. And he had a plan. Not an especially good one. But it was the best that he had been able to come up with at such short notice. He would attempt to negotiate with the kidnapper and free Kayla. If negotiations failed, he'd killed the SOB who had taken her.

Cash kept moving. And saw more blood.

These weren't just drops but smears as if someone had maybe stepped in it while on the move. Perhaps while running to try to escape. The sight of it tightened his gut even more, and he had to shut down the thoughts that the worst had already happened.

Again.

That déjà vu shit was kicking in again.

Cash just kept walking, letting the blood lead him to a room at the end of the hall and to an open door. Kayla's bedroom, he knew. He hadn't actually been inside it, but he'd glanced in it once when he'd visited her here a year ago to exchange Christmas presents.

The lights were off in the room, but the curtains and blinds were both fully open on the trio of floor-to-ceiling windows. There was enough moonlight filtering in through the trio of windows to provide some illumination.

And some damn creepy effects.

Kayla's house was way out in the sticks on acres of ranch land jammed with trees. Some smack dab right outside the windows. That moonlight was spearing through the winter-bare branches and creating a sort of spooky-assed shadow puppet show of skeletal fingers reaching out for him. Those shadow fingers skittered and snaked over the walls, bed, and floor.

Bringing up his gun and steeling himself for an attack from the kidnapper, Cash stepped into the bedroom and immediately whirled to his right when he heard the muffled sound.

"Hell," he spat out.

Kayla.

She was slumping sideways in the doorway of a walk-in closet that was pitch black. Cash couldn't tell if there was anyone behind her. But he had no trouble seeing her face. The fear.

Oh, and that blasted blood.

Along with it being splattered pretty much everywhere on her clothes and hands, it was streaming down the side of her head and smeared into her blonde hair. She had a strip of duct tape over her mouth, and there were plastic cuffs securing her wrists. Despite the cuffs, she was holding something.

A Bowie knife.

The blade was glistening with more blood.

Cash hurried to her, dropping down on his knees beside her and pulling off that tape from her mouth while he continued to keep watch around them. "You're hurt," he blurted.

She muttered his name, and the tears spilling down her cheek cut through the blood. "I knew you'd come," she muttered on a rise of breath. There was both hope and desperate worry in that whisper.

Of course, he'd come. He would have literally walked through fire and anything else to get to her.

"Who did this to you?" he asked, easing the knife from her grip so he could use it to free her from the plastic cuffs.

Kayla was trembling when she tipped her head to the pitch darkness behind her. *Shit.* Was the kidnapper right here, hiding and waiting to strike?

Hoping he wasn't hurting her more than she already was, Cash took hold of Kayla's arm and dragged her out of the closet doorway and into the bedroom, positioning himself between her and whatever monster was inside.

With the fury of a million fires raging through him, he felt around the closet wall for the light switch, knowing that he was destroying what was essentially a crime scene, and he didn't care. Cash had one goal—to deal with the sonofabitch who'd done this to Kayla.

He finally located the switch, flipping it so hard that it probably came close to breaking, and the overhead light flared on, blinding him at first. But not for long. His vision quickly adjusted, and what he saw first was the spray of blood. It was every damn where. On the clothes hanging on each side, the carpet, the walls. Even on the ceiling.

Cash had no trouble figuring out the source.

A man dressed in a blood-drenched Santa suit was sprawled out on the floor. And this Santa was very much dead.

★☆★

CHAPTER TWO

———— ★☆★ ————

Because Kayla knew that Cash was watching her, she tried not to wince as the ER nurse continued to stitch the cut on her head. Cash no doubt already had enough concerns about her, and she didn't want to add more.

She failed.

The wince came anyway, coupled with a sharp sound of pain, and, yeah, Cash noticed, thanks to his amazing ability to multitask. He was talking to two county cops while keeping an eye on both her and the door to the examination room. Judging from the way he kept glancing at that door, he seemed to be anticipating another attack.

Kayla prayed not.

One nightmare at a time was all she could handle, and she was still recovering from this latest one.

Recovery might take more than a while, considering she'd apparently killed a man. Of course, said man had been attempting to murder her at the time, so it wasn't as if she'd had choice about doing what she'd done. Still, she'd killed a human being, and that wasn't going away anytime soon.

Cash wouldn't either.

Despite their pasts—and what a hell of a shared past it was—he had shown up to face down a kidnapper and rescue her. And he'd done that with no backup. He'd just charged right in, ready to save the day. Or rather the night. What he hadn't known was that seconds earlier she'd already ended her kidnapper's life.

Yes, it was going to take much more than a minute or two to process all of that.

She could still hear the sound of the knife stabbing into flesh. Could feel the hot spray of the man's blood. She could still smell that blood even though she was no longer wearing the clothes she'd had on during the attack. The medical staff had taken those, bagging them for the cops to examine, and they'd helped her dress into a pair of green scrubs.

"All done," the nurse finally said, and the woman immediately turned toward Cash and the two cops. "You can talk to her now, but go easy on her, okay?"

"How bad is her injury?" Cash immediately asked.

"Not too bad," the nurse replied. "But someone obviously hit her pretty hard on the head. No concussion, but she'll either need to be admitted for observation or someone will have to stay with her the rest of the night. Whoever stays with her will have to wake her up every two to three hours to make sure she's all right."

Kayla's gaze flew to his, ready to plead for no

hospital admission, but no pleading was required.

"I'll stay with her," Cash insisted before Kayla could speak. "She has this thing about hospitals."

"I hate them," Kayla spoke up. That put some alarm in the nurse's eyes. and to avoid any kind of further examination, she added. "I had a bad experience as a teenager."

Which was the understatement in the history of understatements. But the explanation seemed to satisfy the nurse, and she walked away, leaving Kayla to Cash and the cops.

"I'm County Deputy Aaron Anderson," the older one said. He was tall, lanky and was sporting a little rhinestone Santa pin over his badge. "We're gonna need a full statement as to what happened, but that can wait until you come into the station in the morning. For now, just give us the big picture for our preliminary report."

Kayla nodded, gathering her thoughts. And her breath. It seemed to be lodged in her throat and wasn't budging. Cash noticed that, too. Maybe because she had some panic on her face. He moved closer, sitting on the exam table next to her, and he took hold of her hand.

Which still had blood stains on it.

A sickening mix of hers and the man she'd killed.

She turned her gaze from the blood and focused on just Cash. Not the past. Not the shitty shared memories. Just Cash.

And she started that preliminary report.

"I was in my workshop behind my house. I make custom furniture," Kayla explained. "And while I was doing a final polish on a table, I heard someone running outside. Labored breath, footsteps. My nearest neighbors are about a quarter of a mile away, but I thought maybe something had happened to one of them, so I threw open the door." She paused. Had to. "There was a guy in Santa suit, and he immediately hit me with a stun gun."

She used her free hand to point to her chest, and Kayla lowered the scrub top a couple of inches to show them the burn marks. Deputy Anderson used his phone to photograph it.

"I fell," she went on once she had enough breath to speak. "And I hit my head on the doorframe." Kayla pointed to the fresh stitches on her head, and the deputy photographed that, too.

"Did you recognize the man?" the second deputy asked. According to his name tag, he was Mickey Reeves. He was a good four inches shorter than his partner and looked considerably younger.

Kayla shook her head and winced again at the movement. "No. I didn't know who he was. The beard and the white wig covered most of his face, and he was wearing tinted glasses over his eyes. While I was unable to move or speak, he put the plastic things on my wrists and covered my mouth with duct tape," she spelled out, trying to tamp down her heart that was starting to race again. "Then, he hoisted me over his shoulder and carried me across the backyard and into my house."

"Did he say anything to you when he was doing all of this?" Deputy Anderson asked.

"No. He never spoke a word, but once he had me gagged and cuffed, I saw a text that he was sending to Cash."

"I received it," Cash added, and he took out his phone and showed her the text. The deputies had apparently already seen it because they didn't look at it or snap a photo of it.

Come alone. No cops. No Maverick Ops buddies. Bring 50K to 614 Shelter Lane by midnight or Kayla Morgan dies.

Seeing the words again felt like multiple punches to her stomach. It would have been so easy for her to slide right back into the fear and panic. So damn easy. But Kayla fought it. She needed to finish her statement so she could get the heck out of there and fall apart in private.

"After the man sent the text," she managed to continue, "he started smashing things in my living room. Everything," Kayla emphasized. "I still couldn't move, so I couldn't stop him, and I was bleeding a lot from where I hit my head. But slowly the effects of the stun gun started wearing off, and I saw one of the presents he'd smashed. A Bowie knife in a leather sheath. I grabbed it from the floor and managed to get it out of the sheath before he turned around and saw me."

Once again, she had to stop. Had to fight the fresh

nightmarish images that were playing havoc with the old ones.

"I tried to stab him, but he dodged me," she said, just letting the explanation tumble out of her mouth. *Say it fast. Get this done.* "So, I ran toward my bedroom. I thought if I could get in and lock the door, then I could maybe get to a gun I keep it in my nightstand. I didn't make it that far, though. He cornered me, shoving me in the closet, and that's when I stabbed him."

"Where did you stab him?" Deputy Reeves asked.

She motioned toward her own neck. "I must have hit his carotid artery because blood spurted everywhere. He fell almost immediately, and that's when I got around him. I was still planning to get to my gun. But I collapsed. Couldn't move." Kayla glanced at Cash. "And that's when he came in."

Her gaze met Cash's, and while she saw plenty of concern in his stormy gray eyes, she also saw something else. Something bad. Not the old forbidden heat that was always between them. This was something else that Kayla was absolutely certain she wouldn't want to hear.

"No," she muttered, making another attempt to steel herself up. "Other than the obvious, what's wrong?"

A muscle flickered in Cash's jaw. "The dead guy in the Santa suit is Alvin Parker. He's Virgil Parker's brother."

"Shit," Kayla blurted, and she bolted off the exam

table, ready to run. Where exactly she didn't know. But just hearing Virgil's name gave her a jolt of pure, raw panic.

And memories.

"Cash filled us in on your history with Virgil Parker," Anderson said, the tension loud and clear in his voice. "He attempted to kidnap you and your twin, Kira, when you were fifteen."

"Virgil killed my sister," Kayla heard herself say. Her voice sounded thin, as if it'd come from far, far away.

Both cops nodded. "I pulled up the case file on my phone while you were being examined," Anderson explained. "Virgil was a handyman at your father's construction company in San Antonio. He developed an obsession with you and your sister, but Cash stopped him from taking you—"

Kayla held up her hand. "Uh, I'd rather not hear the details repeated. I'm barely hanging on here," she admitted.

"Of course," Anderson muttered. He put away his phone and shifted his attention to Cash. "You'll bring her to the station in the morning so we can get official statements from both of you?"

Cash made a sound of agreement, and added a thanks and a goodbye as the deputies walked away.

"Just sit here for a moment," Cash told her, helping her back on the exam table. "We have to wait for some paperwork anyway, and that'll give you some time to catch your breath."

Good. Kayla wanted to wait. Wanted to do anything that prevented her from moving. Or thinking. Too bad there was nothing she could do about the latter. The thoughts were coming.

Mercy, were they.

They were coming right at her, slamming into her and weakening that fragile hold she had on the rising panic.

"Did Virgil put his brother, Alvin, up to coming after me?" she asked, trying to anchor herself with the question. And the sound of Cash's voice.

"No. While you were being stitched up, I learned that Virgil died yesterday from injuries he got in a fight at the prison."

Despite everything, the relief came. The wonderful relief of her knowing that her sister's killer was finally dead. Virgil had at last paid for what he'd done. Of course, that hadn't stopped more violence.

In fact, maybe it had caused just the opposite.

"Did Alvin come after me because his brother was killed?" Kayla had to know.

Cash sighed. Nodded. "Yes. I think that's what triggered him."

She laughed, but there was absolutely no humor in it. "Well, Alvin has harassed me over the past twenty years. His son, Harvin, too."

Though Harvin's harassment had only happened with a few ugly social media posts and not the phone calls and in her face visits that Alvin had made to her store. Those had been extreme enough for Kayla to buy a gun and get a restraining order against the man.

Her gaze whipped to Cash again, and Kayla felt yet a new round of the fresh alarm. "Harvin," she managed to say. "Will he come after me now that I killed his father?"

Cash didn't give her a BS assurance about that not happening. Because he couldn't. "You'll take precautions," was what he said instead. "Ruby's trying to track down Harvin now."

Ruby, his boss, as in Ruby Maverick, the kickass leader of an equally kickass Maverick Ops team of security and protection specialists. She would have the resources to find Harvin, maybe before he could arrange an attack against her.

"I know that you being around me triggers the nightmares," he said. "And the panic attacks." Cash pulled in a long, weary breath. "But until we know Harvin's intentions, I need to stay close to you."

Yes, being around him had, and did, cause those things. And more. That blasted heat for one thing.

That heat had started from the moment her body had made her aware of such things when she was thirteen. It had continued the next two years, building and building as Cash and she had their first kiss. Then, more kisses, which had led to making out. They hadn't gone all the way, but they'd been heading in that direction before their lives had been ripped to pieces.

The nightmarish memories and flashbacks had survived for almost twenty years. And so had that heat. Normally, lust was a fun, exciting thing, but not in their case. Because every moment was a reminder of that godawful night. A reminder of losing Kira.

Over the past two decades, Cash and she had attempted to resist the fierce attraction, but once —on her 21st birthday—they'd gotten drunk and landed in bed for some incredible sex.

And her first full-blown panic attack.

That had happened shortly afterward and had been so horrific that Kayla had required hospitalization, and it'd convinced Cash and her that they should keep their hands, and other body parts, off each other. They had succeeded at that, for the most part, anyway.

Until tonight.

He was holding her hand now. Was right next to her. And evidently they were going to be sharing close quarters for a while.

"It's sort of because of you that I got away from Alvin," she heard herself say. She was babbling, and this was one notch above small talk, but she wanted to fill the silence. Because if she didn't, Kayla had learned the hard way that the silence would fill itself with panic. "The Bowie knife I used is...it was supposed to be your Christmas gift."

The corner of his mouth lifted in a near smile. "Nice gift. Thanks."

"I'd planned on dropping it off at Maverick Ops' headquarters first thing in the morning since Christmas is only two days away."

She stopped, considered the time. It was already morning. Three AM to be exact, and since it was December 24th, Christmas was tomorrow.

"I shipped your gift to your store," he let her know, and that sounded like small talk, too. "I figured you'd go there before Christmas."

She would have. In fact, Kayla went there nearly every day, even though she had staff to run the place. Still, she enjoyed just walking around, seeing her own finished work and the pieces of custom furniture that were on consignment from other artisans.

Kayla looked at Cash again, their gazes locking, and the silence returned. So did the wave of emotions, and while she tried to hold back the sob, she wasn't successful. Tears filled her eyes, and her breath shattered.

Cash sighed and eased his arm around her, pulling her to him, but she felt his muscles stiffen. Felt the hesitation over what he was doing. However, no panic came. Only the comfort, and Kayla found herself sliding right into it. She dropped her head on his shoulder and let the tears fall.

They sat there with Cash holding her. He didn't offer up any solutions. Didn't try to fix this. Probably because he knew he couldn't. He just let her cry it out.

With the fresh round of tears came the bone-weary exhaustion from the ordeal and the spent adrenaline. Kayla might have drifted off to sleep then and there, but his phone buzzed, the sound echoing through the room.

"Sorry," he muttered, taking out his cell from his pocket. "It's Maverick Ops' headquarters," Cash let her know.

He answered it, and while he didn't put the call on speaker, Kayla had no trouble hearing what the caller said because she kept her head on his shoulder and right against his ear.

"This is Tammy at dispatch. Cash, someone just called here asking to speak to you. He says he's Harvin Parker."

That got her head whipping up from his shoulder. Kayla practically snapped to attention, and her gaze flew to Cash's.

"I know Ruby's looking for this guy," the dispatcher went on, "so I'll alert her about this."

"Put the call through to my phone," Cash instructed, and while he waited, he switched to speaker mode.

Kayla immediately started trying to steel herself up for what she might hear. But there wasn't a lot of time to do that. Barely a couple of seconds before she heard the man's voice.

"Cash," he said, his voice tight with rage. "And I'm guessing that Kayla's listening. If not, pass along this message to her. Soon, she'll pay for what she's done to my father. Soon, the murdering bitch will be dead."

★☆★

CHAPTER THREE

———— ★☆★ ————

Cash threaded his SUV around the sharp curves of the rural road toward his house. Like Kayla's, his place was nowhere near the proverbial beaten path, and at this hour, there was no other traffic.

Well, none of that he saw anyway.

But he kept watch for Harvin just in case the asshole was already lying in wait. Not a lot of people knew where Cash lived, but with all the digital tools and internet resources available, it wouldn't be hard for Harvin to get the info. Nor would it be hard for Harvin to assume that Cash would be taking Kayla to his place.

That last possibility was giving Cash plenty of concern and having him second guess this, but Kayla was exhausted and in pain. And his house was more secure than a hotel would be.

Far more.

After all, one of the benefits of working for Ruby Maverick was that the operatives got all the current bells and whistles when it came to security and threat detection.

Despite the exhaustion and pain, Kayla wasn't sleeping. She was sitting straight in the seat as if on alert. And she probably was. It'd be impossible for her to fully relax after the shit that she'd been through tonight. Cash wished it was over, that she wasn't still in danger, but Harvin's phone call had made it clear that she was the target.

Yeah.

Harvin apparently intended to pick up where his father and uncle left off. Or rather try to do that anyway. Cash intended to end the miserable SOB's life before he could get to Kayla. He'd failed to protect her sister all those years ago, and he had no desire to put her through that kind of hell again.

"What made you move out here to the Hill Country?" Kayla asked, the question cutting through the flood of thoughts and worries going through his head. "I mean, other that the fact it's beautiful."

It was indeed beautiful. A Texas paradise with its rolling hills and, in the spring, acres of the famous bluebonnets. Along with that were the limestone bluffs, mineral springs, and a nice side dish of peace and quiet. It was even quieter in winter, especially now with the glistening frost covering the ground.

"Ruby had some houses built out here for her operatives, and I bought one of them," he explained as he took the final turn to his house. It was a private road with sensors that started to ping the app on his phone.

"Gunner," Cash instructed the app. "I'm driving

through. Keep the sensors activated."

Despite the annoying pings that jacked up his adrenaline and caused his body to automatically brace for a fight, Cash didn't want to turn them off in case Harvin was nearby, ready to strike. The asshole could try to use their arrival to sneak onto the property.

"Gunner?" she repeated.

"That's what I call the app that manages the security system along with pretty much the rest of the place," he explained. "And, yes, it's named after the dog I had when I was a kid."

Kayla smiled. "I remember. A German Shepherd. He once ate my ice cream cone, and I cried."

Cash remembered that. Remembered, too, using his entire meager savings to buy her another one. He'd enjoyed watching her eat that cone.

Hell, he'd enjoyed most of his time with Kayla.

They'd met when he was eight and she had been seven. That was the summer his folks had bought the house next to her parents, and along with Kira, they'd become fast playmates.

And something else.

Even though Cash had been just a kid, he had felt an instant connection with Kayla. Friendship at first sight, but later, when his brain had been better able to process such things, it had felt more like...well, that she was his soulmate.

Oh, he'd mentally kicked his own ass over that flowery label.

But while he disapproved of the word itself, the feeling remained. And was still there.

It was ironic that he'd never had that kind of connection with Kira despite her being Kayla's identical twin. Cash had always been able to tell them apart, unlike just about everyone else in the neighborhood, and when he'd become a teenager, it'd been Kayla he'd had wet dreams about.

Then, things had gone to hell when they were fifteen. Virgil had launched that hell by acting on this obsession with them and trying to abduct the girls at knifepoint.

Even now, those images were way too fresh. One week before Christmas. There'd been the threat of frost and maybe even some rare snow with the temps dropping into the low thirties. And there had been the lingering smell of the smoke from the neighbors' fireplaces. Central Texas didn't always get winter weather when the rest of the country did, but it had that night.

Christmas lights and decorations were everywhere. Lots of blinking colors and so much anticipation of the holiday. Or rather the Christmas party that Kayla, Kira, and he had been invited to. Their parents were already at one just up the street, but this was a party just for the teenagers in the neighborhood. A costume deal where Cash had been planning to make out with Kayla and ogle her in the fairly skimpy Mrs. Santa costume she'd already modeled for him.

Cash had opted for a Santa suit, a cheap one he'd bought from a party supply store. Staying with the Christmas theme, Kira was going as an elf.

As planned, Cash had dropped by Kayla's house at eight so Kira and they could walk to the party together. But when he got there, Virgil already had a knife to Kira's throat and was using it to force both Kayla and her toward his car in the side driveway. Cash had seen the look in the man's eyes and knew one thing.

They were the eyes of a killer.

Kayla's head was bleeding, and Cash had learned later that Virgil had clubbed her with the handle of his knife. He'd punched her, too, and broken a couple of her ribs when she'd tried to fight back. She had only surrendered and submitted when Virgil had put the knife to Kira's throat.

That night, Cash hadn't paused to think about Kayla's injuries. The knife. Or anything else other than getting to the girls and saving them. Shouting for help but sure as hell not waiting for it, he'd grabbed a handful of rocks and tried to pelt Virgil with them. When that hadn't worked, Cash had lunged at him.

And failed at that, too.

He'd managed to yank Kayla away from Virgil and sling her behind him. But before Cash could do the same to Kira, Virgil had jabbed the knife into her not once but three times. By then, the neighbors had run to help and had restrained Virgil, but it had been too late.

Kira was dead.

That was an image that was the clearest of them all. Kira, lifeless and bleeding on the cold ground, and Kayla sobbing over her body.

Thankfully, that image didn't freeze in his mind as it sometimes did because Gunner's voice cut through the mental noise.

"Should I open the garage door for you and your visitor?" the app said.

"Yes," Cash verified.

"How did Gunner know you had someone with you?" Kayla asked.

"I have security cameras and infrared sensors all over the property. I'll get plenty of advance notice if someone approaches."

Of course, that wouldn't stop a sniper from shooting through the windows, but Cash would take precautions for that, too.

He pulled into the garage and turned off the engine, but he didn't get out until the garage door had fully closed. Kayla was still struggling with her seatbelt by the time he made it to the passenger's side, and he helped her with that, being careful not to touch her too much, then he led her inside.

As programmed, the lights came on, and the door automatically locked behind them. *Kryptonite* by 3 Doors Down started to blare out from the hidden speakers. Again, that was usual. But Cash shut it down with a simple voice command. Kayla's raw nerves probably didn't need his blaring music. Or so he thought.

"Keep it on," she insisted.

Cash did, but he instructed Gunner to lower the volume. Along with lowering the shutters on the entire house. A security measure to prevent someone from spotting them through the windows. Around them, merging with the now softer playing music, there was the whirring sounds of the shutters.

"If you're hungry," he said, motioning for her to follow him out of the mudroom and into the kitchen. "I can fix you—"

"No. I can't eat anything," she muttered while she glanced around the great room, that was the living, dining, and kitchen area.

When Ruby had had the place built, she'd gone for a neutral palate, and Cash hadn't made a whole lot of changes. The basic décor was white with varying shades of a pale, watery blue and green for the walls, rugs, and furniture. His one contribution was the dining table and chairs that he had purchased shortly after he'd moved in.

And Kayla spotted that purchase.

Her attention landed on the rich oak table with the live edges that incorporated the shape and natural elements of the wood. Both it and the chairs had obviously been made by a highly skilled craftsman and were works of art.

And Kayla herself was the artist.

"You bought some of my pieces," she said,

sounding more than a little surprised. She ran her hand along the table. "I mean, I knew someone had bought it, but it was a cash purchase, so I didn't know who."

He hadn't wanted her to know. Hadn't wanted her to think of him and spiral into panic again. But he could see now that he'd been wrong to assume that. Kayla seemed pleased.

"You do good work," he let her know.

"Thanks. I had a good teacher."

Her dad. He had indeed introduced Kayla to his hobby, and she'd turned into something much more. Cash didn't know what her net worth was, but he knew she had a very successful business. One that gave her all the solitude and privacy she needed.

Until a few hours ago, anyway.

Alvin might have permanently snatched that solitude away, though by attacking her in her workshop. Cash hoped that when this was over, when Harvin was caught and neutralized, that Kayla would be able to go back to the work she clearly loved without the memories of Alvin's attack.

Kayla walked into the living room, glancing at the framed photos on his mantel. Some of his late folks. Some of him with friends and colleagues.

And the one of her.

Cash cursed for not getting the chance to remove it. It was a photo of them at age fifteen at one of her dad's barbecues. The summer before Kira's death. Before life as they'd known it had gone to hell in a really shitty handbasket.

In the shot, Cash had his arm slung around her neck. A neck that sported a hickey from one of their making out sessions. They were both grinning like loons and probably having trashy thoughts about each other.

"I'm glad you kept that picture," she said, surprising him.

In the past, when they'd touched on, well, the past, she'd shut it quickly down. Maybe this was the fatigue talking.

"I kept my copy of the picture, too. But..." She stopped, turned to face him.

And there it was. She was shutting down the godawful memories.

"Thank you for saving me," Kayla said, and then added a muttered, "*again*. You do know that Alvin sent you that text to get you to my place so he could kill both of us?"

Cash nodded. Yeah, he'd known that, but the man couldn't have issued any threat that would have stopped him from trying to rescue her. But as it turned out, she'd already rescued herself.

Which brought him to the blood.

It was still on her hands and in her hair. And Cash was about to show her the guestroom so she could shower, but she walked toward the corner of the living room and frowned when she spotted the undecorated tree and the boxes of ornaments on the floor.

"I haven't gotten around to decorating," he murmured, and he likely wouldn't now that it was Christmas Eve. Especially not, too, with Harvin's threat looming over them.

But it was more than that. And he confessed that to Kayla.

"Except when I was away on deployment, every year I get a tree and drag out that box of lights and ornaments, but I managed to finish it."

She nodded. "It was the same for me until a couple of years ago. It didn't feel right putting up stuff when Kira wasn't around to enjoy it. Plus, my folks weren't around either."

Yeah, that was it, along with just the sight of the decorations triggering the bad memories. For Kayla, it was probably a double hit since her parents had died in a car crash around the holidays when she'd been twenty-four.

Cash totally understood. His parents were gone, too. First, his mom from cancer the year he'd finished high school. His dad had pretty much checked out of life after that and had passed away from a heart attack when Cash had been on his first deployment. Without parents or siblings around, the holidays could be tough, even without the addition of the crap nightmare Virgil had given them.

"But after more therapy, I realized that the tree could be like a tribute to Kira," Kayla went on. "She loved Christmas."

She had indeed, and Kira had been even more

excited about going to that party than even Cash had been.

"Well, at least you have that decoration up." She pointed to a cheesy-looking Santa in a hula skirt, shorts, and flip-flops holding up two bottles of tequila.

Cash smiled. "A gift from one of my co-workers. Jericho. He, uh, has a strange sense of humor."

Kayla attempted a smile, too. It didn't come close to looking genuine, and it really stood no chance whatsoever of forming once she glanced down at her bloody hands.

"This way," he insisted, motioning for her to follow him to the hall. He led her to the guestroom and pointed at the ensuite bathroom. "The shower's in there."

Kayla nodded and glanced at the bathroom. Then, the bed. "I don't want to sleep alone," she blurted.

The tremble in her voice got to him. So did that haunted look in her eyes. Hell. That bastard Alvin and his spawn had spun her back twenty years to that nightmare she'd barely survived.

Cash swallowed hard. "You won't be alone." He pointed to a chair in the corner. "I'll be there."

"That doesn't look very comfortable," she remarked.

It wouldn't be, but Cash wasn't expecting to get much sleep anyway. "I'll be fine," he assured her. That was true about the sleeping arrangements, but everything else was in the shitstorm mode.

Including his feelings for Kayla.

It was damn hard to be around her and not touch or want her. In fact, the not wanting was impossible. But he'd keep his distance, somehow.

Kayla didn't, though.

On a heavy sigh, she went to him and pulled him into her arms. Her body landed against his, and she didn't jump back as if he'd scalded her.

Cash listened for any changes in her breathing. Any signs that she was about to have a panic attack. Thank God there weren't any. She just stood there, holding him while he held her.

After several minutes, she finally eased back, and their gazes locked. Hell. The heat came. So damn much of it. But he didn't kiss her. Cash's arms slid away from her as she moved back even more. Still, she didn't seem to be retreating in terror from the flashbacks.

"Shower," she muttered. "I'll make sure not to get my stitches wet." After giving him one last look, she headed in that direction.

Cash didn't curse until she'd shut the door and could no longer hear him. He was about to launch into a stern lecture to himself about his hands-off policy with Kayla, but before he could do that, his phone buzzed.

Ruby's name flashed on the screen.

Obviously, his boss wasn't getting any more sleep or rest than Kayla and he were, but he prayed she was calling with good news.

"Did you find Harvin?" he immediately asked.

"No," Ruby was quick to reply. "But I know what he's been up to, and, Cash, it's not good. He just posted this on the dark web."

Shit. Cash definitely didn't like the sound of that. However, before he could question Ruby about it, his phone dinged with the sound of an incoming video, and he clicked on it.

It was grainy footage but still clear enough for Cash to see the man dressed in a Santa suit. He was on his knees in what appeared to be some kind of warehouse. At first he thought it was Harvin mimicking his dad's choice of costumes, but then Cash spotted someone behind the Santa.

Harvin himself.

There was no doubting it, and while Harvin was looking directly in the camera, he kept a gun pointed at the Santa.

"This message is for the murdering bitch, Kayla, and the Maverick Ops' fucker who keeps saving her sorry ass," Harvin growled. "Come to me and surrender, both of you, or this will just keep on happening."

And with that, Harvin pulled the trigger.

★☆★

CHAPTER FOUR

———— ★☆★ ————

Kayla woke up in pain. Her head was throbbing, and every muscle in her body seemed to be twisted and knotted, screaming for her to move and try to untangle them. It was like a dozen Charley horses going on at once.

She jackknifed to a sitting position. And instantly regretted doing that. The sudden movement made the pain so much worse, and she gasped to try to catch her breath.

"It's okay," someone said.

Cash.

He was right there, easing to sit down on the bed next to her. His weight shifted the soft mattress so that she slid against him.

She latched onto the sound of his voice, his face, his scent, using all of those things to ground her and bring her back from the pain. It worked. It worked even better when he took hold of her hand.

No panic came rushing over her. Just the opposite. His touch was more effective than those other three things had been.

Well, almost.

Panic was rarely her default when she caught a glimpse of his face. And what a face it was. When she'd been a teenager, she had thought Cash was the hottest guy she'd ever seen.

And he still was.

That black hair, stubble, and piercing gray eyes hit all the right notes. His body did, too. Not overly muscled, just toned and perfect.

Yes, Cash still had her hormonal number despite all the other stuff that happened when he touched her. Correction—the stuff that *usually* happened when he touched her. The panic and the flood of memories of Kira's murder. But all of that wasn't rearing its ugly head now. Nor had it when they'd been at the hospital.

"The hospital," she repeated aloud now that she had some breath.

She wasn't there in the ER, and it took her brain a couple of seconds to catch up. She had been treated at the county hospital and released, and Cash had brought her to his place. She had showered, changed into one of his t-shirts and a pair of his boxers, and he had helped her to bed in his guest room. A very dark guest room with the curtains closed and the only light coming from the slightly ajar door of the bathroom.

During the night, Cash had woken her several times, asking her to tell him her name or his. That was a blur in her mind now, and she'd been able to fall right back to sleep. But he'd done that to follow the nurse's orders, to make sure she was all right.

That mental recap had Kayla searching for the time, and she finally saw it on Cash's watch. Nine AM.

"Good grief," she muttered, trying to push the hair out of her eyes without touching the stitches. "I slept longer than I thought I would."

"I'm glad you did. You needed it." He glanced at the bandage on her forehead. "You also need some pain meds."

It wasn't a question, and he was one hundred percent correct. Cash immediately reached over to the nightstand and took two tablets from a bottle of some extra-strength over-the-counter meds. He handed them to her along with the glass of water that he had ready and waiting.

Kayla gulped them down while she studied him. That hot face could definitely be a distraction, but she could still see the worry in his eyes.

And maybe something else.

"You'll need to eat," Cash insisted before she could ask him about that *something else*.

He took hold of her hand again, his grip ever so light, and he eased her out of the bed and to her feet. Thankfully, his t-shirt was huge on her and went halfway down her thighs. Not that she would have been overly concerned about modesty right now, but she also didn't want to try to have breakfast while she was half-naked.

Despite the hours of sleep, she still felt sluggish

and slow as if she were walking through thick syrup. Cash helped with that, too, by leading her into his kitchen and having her sit at the counter.

There was the strong scent of coffee in the air, and she spotted a half full pot of it sitting in the fancy-looking stainless steel maker.

"Juice and toast for starters?" he asked.

She nodded, and her stomach must have also heard the question because it growled, causing Cash to smile.

"Maybe some scrambled eggs, too," he added.

That actually sounded good, and Kayla couldn't recall the last time she'd eaten. "I wouldn't say no to coffee," she let him know.

He poured her a huge mug of it, and with his back to her, he got to work prepping her breakfast.

"Have they found Harvin?" she asked.

Cash shook his head. "Not yet. Ruby's got a full team working on finding him."

She wished he'd been looking at her when he said that. Then, she might know if their not having located Harvin was the reason she was getting this vibe from him. A vibe that he was holding onto some bad news.

Kayla downed enough coffee to give her a nice jolt of caffeine, and it also seemed to help with her headache. She sipped some more before she stood, went around the counter and stopped right next to Cash.

He looked down at her, and she didn't think it

was her imagination that he seemed to be steeling himself up for something. "I'm sorry," he murmured.

The apology confused her, and maybe it was the mix of everything—the pain, the worry, the fear—but Kayla found herself setting her coffee mug aside and moving even closer to him.

Then closer still until she stepped into his arms.

Behind them, she heard the toast pop up, but neither of them moved. Not at first, anyway. Slowly, gently, Cash's arms finally came around her.

Both of them sighed. His seemed to be a mixed bag of comfort and attraction. Hers had some of the same, but there was also relief. She felt a lot of things, but thank sweet heaven, panic wasn't on the emotional radar.

She stayed there, letting him soothe her. And arouse her. It'd been a while since she had felt this strong pull. Fast and hot. Probably fueled by, well, everything else, but it was a nice buzz that she wanted to hang onto for a moment. Much better than the other stuff she'd been feeling.

"We're playing with fire," he let her know.

They were. That didn't have her moving away either. But she did move. Kayla leaned back her head enough that she could look him in the eyes. Still, no panic. Just the exact opposite.

And that fast and hot tug in her body just kept on going.

Before she even knew she was going to do it, she came up on her toes and brushed her mouth against his. Definitely playing with fire, and that buzz went wild, sliding through her body, straight to her center. Kayla would have added some pressure to that kiss. She would have turned it into a real one. Long, deep, and filled with the need building inside her.

But it was Cash who stopped it.

He took hold of her shoulders, and this time, the eye contact wasn't a lust-filled gaze. She saw that *something else* again. The bad news.

And this time, she got out the question she needed to ask. "What's wrong?"

Cash didn't jump to answer. Not a good sign. Added to that, he pulled in a long breath. "Ruby found something on the dark web. Live feed from a staged scene. It was Harvin," he added a heartbeat later.

She shook her head. "But you said you didn't know where he was."

"We don't. The live feed was from a concealed IP address." Another pause. Another breath. "The feed was a message for us. Harvin wants us to surrender to him."

A burst of air left her mouth. A laugh but not from humor. "And why does he think we'd do that?"

Cash didn't dodge her gaze this time. "During the live feed, he shot a man wearing a Santa suit, and Harvin said he'd shoot others if you and I didn't surrender."

Oh, God.

Kayla's breath vanished, and she would have

staggered back if Cash hadn't kept his grip on her shoulders. Now, the panic did come, and she had to fight to stomp it down. Had to fight, too, just to think this through.

"It could have been a hoax," she managed to say. "Harvin could have shot the man with blanks."

Cash was quick to shake his head. "At the end of the live feed, Harvin said where the cops could find the body. They responded right away, but by the time they got there, Harvin was gone, and they found the man dead from a single gunshot wound to the head."

Kayla let each word of that sink in. It didn't sink in well, and she moved out of Cash's grip so she could sink down onto the floor. She sat, anchoring her back against the island while she tried to regain... everything.

"The dead man has been IDed," Cash went on, "and he appears to have no direct connection to Harvin and his shitbag gene pool. The guy was heading to a costume party at a bar, and according to the security camera feed, he was abducted at gunpoint in the parking lot."

So, he was someone out for a night of fun, and Harvin had ended his life even though the man had had nothing to do with Alvin's and Virgil's deaths.

"You've seen a recording of the shooting?" she asked.

"I have," he confirmed. But he didn't add more. Wouldn't. He was trying to protect her again.

"I want to see the feed," she muttered.

Cash gave a heavy sigh and sank down on the floor next to her. "No, you don't. And I'm not going to show it to you. There's no reason for you to have that in your head."

Kayla could have said she was mentally seeing it all anyway. And she was. But viewing it wouldn't be just a gut punch for herself but another one for Cash as well. Besides, by now Cash, Ruby, and the Maverick Ops' techs had no doubt examined and reexamined every frame of it while the cops processed the scene for anything they could use to find Harvin.

"So, what do we do?" she came out and asked. "How do we surrender?"

His mouth went tight. "We don't. *You* don't," he amended. Then, he stopped and cursed. "Right now, even if we wanted to hand ourselves over to that asshole, we wouldn't know where to do that. Harvin hasn't spelled out any details."

"But he will." Kayla was certain of that.

You didn't murder a man in a Santa suit, someone who was perhaps even a stranger, unless you were sending a strong message. And that message was that Harvin wanted Cash and her.

"Harvin intends for us to pay for what happened to his father and uncle," Kayla went on. "Ironic, since his father started all of this. And I'm not the least bit sorry that Virgil and Alvin are dead," she tacked onto that.

Cash made a sound of agreement. "Now, we need to let Ruby's team find Harvin so he'll be stopped, too."

That made it sound so simple. So attainable. And clearly it wasn't or they would have already found Harvin.

"Does Harvin have the resources to hide from Maverick Ops?" she asked.

"He has resources," Cash admitted. "His grandparents left him about a quarter of a million two years ago, and he's had extensive firearms and combat training."

"More training than you?" But she waved that off. She doubted anyone had more than Cash in that department.

Since she'd followed his career, she knew he'd been a decorated Navy SEAL and had followed that up with an equally stellar career for Maverick Ops.

"Harvin must be delusional or cocky to go after a former SEAL," Kayla concluded.

"He's both," Cash was quick to admit. "And he's very dangerous. Added to that, we can't exactly put out a warning for anyone in a Santa suit to be careful. It's Christmas Eve."

Cash was right. There'd be hundreds of Santas out and about. No way to protect them all, which meant Harvin likely would have no trouble coming up with his next victim.

Or rather his lure.

Because that's what the next one would likely be. A way to get Cash and her to do that *surrender*.

The next wave of emotions surprised her. Kayla

had figured on some fear, anger, and panic coming along with the threat of death. But other things flashed into her head.

"After I just kissed you, I wasn't thinking about Harvin," she admitted. "Or the past. I was thinking that I might finally be ready to start living again. An actual life without all this baggage and nightmarish smudges."

Kayla didn't say the rest of what she'd been thinking. No, the timing sucked for him to hear all of that. But she had been considering that she wanted that actual life to be with Cash.

The silence came, settling between them. But not for long. His phone buzzed, and Kayla got a fresh sense of dread. The dread went up when he took out his cell from his pocket, and she saw Ruby's name on the screen.

Cash answered it and immediately said, "Ruby, you're on speaker. Kayla is right next to me." He'd no doubt added that in case Ruby could soften whatever she was about to say.

"We just got a call from Harvin," Ruby explained. "He's set up another live feed on the dark web, and he wants Kayla and you to tune in." She paused. "Brace yourself. He has another victim."

★☆★

CHAPTER FIVE

———— ★☆★ ————

Hell. Cash had hoped they'd have more time, that Harvin would have a cooling off period from his last kill. A cooling off that would give Ruby and the Maverick Ops' search team a chance to find the asshole and stop him before he could murder anyone else.

But Harvin apparently wasn't taking a break.

Worse, the sonofabitch wanted everyone, including Kayla and him, to be witnesses. Of course, Harvin intended for them to be much more than mere observers. This live feed was no doubt his way of throwing down the gauntlet. The challenge for Kayla and him to *surrender*.

"Are you willing to talk to Harvin?" Ruby asked.

"I am," Cash said, glancing at Kayla. Of course, she nodded. "We're both willing," he amended.

"Figured as much," Ruby muttered. "I'm sending you the link for the live feed now," she explained. "The techs are already examining it to try to determine location."

Maybe the techs would get lucky with that, but

Cash was betting that Harvin didn't intend to stay in this place for long.

"When you click on the link, block your video," Ruby instructed. "No need to give a killer a visual on Kayla or you."

Yeah, no reason except Harvin might demand it. But Cash would deal with that if and when it happened.

The link popped up on his phone, and Cash had a quick debate as to how to handle this. If he viewed this on the small screen of his phone, he could maybe exclude Kayla from seeing the worst of it.

Or seeing it at all.

He wanted to try to talk Kayla into just keeping her eyes closed, but one look at her face and he knew he would fail at that.

"I want to watch it," Kayla insisted. "I need to hear what he has to say."

Cash did a whole lot of silent cursing and hoped he could undo any damage Kayla would experience from looking at this nightmare.

He went ahead and sent the link to his monitor. The huge Texas landscape painting over the mantel faded, the feed replacing it. Like the other footage, this one was grainy and dark. Not a warehouse this time but rather the interior of a rustic log cabin.

The camera that Harvin was using appeared to be stationary, either sitting on something or on a tripod. The angle didn't shift even a little, an indication that no human was holding it. But clearly a human had focused it—Harvin—and he had aimed it right at him and his stupid grinning face.

The man in the Santa suit sure as hell wasn't smiling. Even with the thick white wig and fake beard, Cash could see the terror in his expression. He was on his knees with Harvin behind him. Like victim one, Harvin had put a gun to this guy's head as well.

The Santa's wrists had also been zip-tied. Probably his feet, too, though Cash couldn't see them. He also had a swatch of duct tape covering his mouth. Had Harvin done that to make sure the guy stayed quiet and wouldn't alert anyone if he started yelling? Or maybe Harvin had known what his father had done to Kayla and was mimicking that.

"Ah, is that the murdering bitch and Maverick Ops' fucker who keeps saving her? Hard to tell since I'm looking at a big-assed blank screen." Harvin taunted. "Tell me if you can hear me."

"We can hear," Cash replied.

Harvin's mouth twisted into a sneer. "And the bitch? Speak up, killer, so I know you're not tucked away in some corner, boo-hooing your eyes out or pissing your panties 'cause you're too damn scared."

Kayla hiked up her chin, and Cash saw the fire in her eyes. Hell. This was better than tears or panic. Even better than fear. But Cash didn't want the anger controlling her emotions now. They both needed to keep a cool head.

"I can hear you," she said, enunciating each word

as if chewing them up and spitting them out. Her fury came through loud and clear.

Probably aware that he had pushed her buttons, Harvin laughed and just kept on pushing. "Cowards, both of you not to even show your faces when I'm showing you mine. And his."

Harvin gave the Santa a hard jab in the temple with his gun, causing the man to make a muffled cry in pain.

"Focus on us, not him," Cash insisted. "He's just a tool you're using to get our attention. Well, you have our attention so you don't need him."

Harvin laughed again, but there wasn't a drop of humor in it. "I need him and others like him to get you two to fully cooperate. Yes, this is a start, and we're nowhere near the finish line."

"Get to the point," Kayla snapped.

The laughter stopped, and Harvin's eyes narrowed. "The point is I'll be burying my father before New Year's, and you, bitch, are responsible for that."

"I don't have to remind you that your father tried to kill Kayla," Cash was quick to respond.

"Noooo," Harvin said, stretching out the response. "He tried to avenge his brother. My Uncle Virgil died in prison."

Kayla huffed. "Here's a history lesson. Your Uncle Virgil murdered my sister while he was trying to abduct us."

Harvin muttered a "Yeah, right" as if he didn't

buy any of that. "Bitch, if you hadn't teased my uncle and led him on, he would have never made a play for you."

Shit. What a warped sense of logic, but there was no telling what stories Alvin had spun to his brother and what had gone on that horrible night.

"I didn't tease your uncle," Kayla insisted, the fury in her voice. "He was a dangerous piece..." She stopped, no doubt realizing that if she pushed Harvin's buttons, then he might just pull the trigger.

Kayla took some deep breaths, making a visible attempt to rein in her emotions. Hard to do with this delusional asshole, but she managed it.

"What do you want?" Kayla asked instead. "How do we stop you from murdering innocent people?"

Harvin got a flash of anger, too. Probably over that *murdering* comment, but he stared right into the camera.

"We'll get into specific location later," he said. "I need to set a few things up first before I'm ready for you two. For now, here are the rules." He held up one finger on his left hand. "Wherever I tell you go, you two come alone. A-l-o-n-e," he spelled out. "If I get a whiff anyone is with you, then you'll get to witness a blood bath. In fact, you'll be a central part of that."

Cash's gut twisted. This SOB was going to involve more than just this one unlucky Santa.

Harvin held up another finger. "Rule two. Bring no guns, and I'll know if you're carrying because I have some nifty equipment to detect that sort of thing." He paused. "But I want the bitch to bring a knife. One big fuckin' knife."

"Why?" Kayla wanted to know.

Harvin grinned. "That's for me to know and you to find out. Oh, and FYI, you'll be finding out the hard way, bitch."

Cash silently cursed. Harvin was going to try to kill her the way his father had died. Of course, he wouldn't let that happen, but without details of the location and the set up, he wasn't sure how he was going to stop this sick game that Harvin had set into motion.

"Gotta go for now," Harvin said in a syrupy sweet voice. "I'll be chatting again with you very, very soon."

A split second before he shut down the feed, Cash heard something that he sure as hell hadn't wanted to hear.

A gunshot.

★☆★

CHAPTER SIX

———— ★☆★ ————

Kayla sat at Cash's dining table and waited for him to finish his latest call with Ruby. She didn't mind the flurry of calls and texts that'd been going on because getting info was vital. Plus, she was using the time to try to settle all the raw nerves zinging through her body.

Even now, a full hour after the live feed with Harvin had ended, the sound of that bullet being fired was echoing in Kayla's head, and it showed no signs of fading. The images were staying with her, too.

She hadn't actually seen the shot blast into the man in the Santa suit, but she had no doubts that Harvin had murdered him.

And for what?

To prove he was a cold-blooded killer and that he meant business? He'd already accomplished that with the first man he'd shot. So, either Harvin just liked killing innocent people or else he wanted to torture Cash and her before the big finale. Perhaps both.

Since that big finale would likely happen soon, she'd changed back into the scrubs that she'd gotten in the ER. Hardly showdown garments, but they would have to do since she didn't want to go back to her place and get her own clothes. Still, that was something she would need to do if this ordeal with Harvin dragged on.

Cash finished his latest call, but he stared at his phone for a couple of seconds before putting it away. Kayla guessed he also needed a moment to settle himself before he relayed anything to her.

"Still no contact from Harvin," he said, making his way to a coat closet.

Except it wasn't an ordinary closet, she realized when he opened the door and she got a look inside. It was more like a mini arsenal with weapons and all sorts of gear. Stuff that he would need for his usual Maverick Ops assignments.

Cash took out two bulletproof vests and some other equipment. Not guns but what appeared to be mini flares.

"These won't show up on a metal scan," Cash said, donning one of the vests and slipping some of the flares into the pockets of his cargo pants. "These produce diffused red light that looks like thick smoke."

That could come in handy to conceal themselves or distract Harvin, and her mind began to spin with all sorts of possibilities for a showdown with a killer. Harvin wasn't going to make this easy for them, but she also believed he'd want to toy with them first. He would want to dole out more of that mental torture. Hopefully, during that, Cash and she could figure out a way to stop Harvin from going after anyone else while Cash and she got out of there alive.

Cash added a communication earpiece to his gear stash before he took something else out of the closet. A slingshot.

"It's from my friend, Jericho," Cash said when he saw the look she was giving him. "He puts it to good use in ops, and again, it won't show up on a metal scan."

"Neither will rocks," she said. "Got any of them in the closet?"

"Something better than rocks." He took out stone arrowheads. They were rounded on the bottom but had two-inch long pointy tips, and he shoved some of those into his pockets as well. So, Cash wouldn't be bringing in any guns, but he would have weapons.

And so would she.

Cash took out a knife. A big one. In fact, it could have probably qualified as a machete. Carrying it, the second vest and what she thought was a neck guard to protect that area of her body from a bullet, he went to her, setting the items on the table as he sank down in the chair next to her.

"Once we know what Harvin has in mind, we can come up with a plan," he muttered.

Kayla thought of the rules that Harvin had laid out. Cash and she had to come alone, and she had to bring a knife. Since Harvin would have a gun, a knife wouldn't be an ideal weapon, but she had no doubts that Ruby and Cash could come up with something to make the situation survivable.

She hoped so anyway.

"We need a plan that doesn't include you going in," Cash amended.

Their gazes locked, and in his eyes she saw the intense determination to keep her safe. "Harvin isn't going to allow any scenario where we're both not there," she spelled out. "I'm the one who killed his father, and he blames both of us for his uncle being in prison."

His jaw went tight, and he cursed under his breath. What he didn't do was admit she was right, which meant he was going to try to keep her out of harm's way while he walked straight to a killer.

Sighing again, she shifted the subject a little. "Have they found the second dead Santa?" she asked.

Cash shook his head. "Not yet. But about twenty minutes after he ended the live feed, Harvin called the cops to give them a location, and they're heading there now. It's an old fishing cabin out on Medina Lake. No close neighbors. No one around to hear the shot and report it."

Harvin had almost certainly factored that in when he'd chosen the location. The man would be doing the same for the one he was setting up for Cash and her. Again, her mind went to all the torturous possibilities the SOB could set up, but that didn't help her breathing or her nerves.

To settle herself, Kayla ran her right hand over the smooth surface of the table. That gave her a jolt of better thoughts, better memories of when she'd been making it.

"It's so funny that you bought this piece because I was thinking of you when I was working on it," she confessed.

He gave her a flat look. "How the heck did you connect me to a table?"

"Not to the table itself but rather the oak slab I used. Wood has its own personality. This one is strong, interesting…and sensual."

His look got flatter, but the corner of mouth lifted slightly in a smile. So, she had accomplished that at least. "Sensual, really?" he asked.

"Absolutely." Keeping her eyes fixed on him, she continued running her hands over the surface. "The grain patterning in this wood is called flame because it looks like a fire. Hot, sensual. Hard."

He fought the smile now. "You know, I can think of a lot of dirty analogies right now."

"Good." Because dirty was better than dwelling on the threat they had hanging over them.

Kayla decided to amp up the dirtiness a bit. She caught onto the front of his vest, pulling Cash closer and closer. Until she could reach his mouth, then, she kissed him.

Mercy.

The jolt was instant, and it was scalding hot.

So hot that Kayla felt herself melting into the kiss. Into Cash. He didn't back down either. Didn't put an immediate stop to it. But he did make a hoarse sound of pleasure, and he hooked his arm around her, drawing her against him.

Of course, it wasn't skin to skin contact. There were a lot of layers between them, but her body seemed especially thrilled to have his chest against hers. That pressure was delicious, but at the moment, the star of this particular dirty show was the kiss.

Cash deepened it, his tongue brushing over hers. That upped the heat even more and shot a wave of lust-filled need through her. When she'd started this kissing, she hadn't thought it could jump forward so darn fast, but she was already thinking of more, more, more.

She was thinking about sex.

The kiss raged on, causing her to ache for him, and Kayla moved onto his lap so her center would be against his. The contact was exactly what her body was clamoring for, and she would have definitely kept it up...if Cash hadn't stopped.

He tore his mouth from hers and took hold of her shoulders.

"Panic attack," he reminded her.

She managed to laugh. "I'm feeling a lot of things, Cash, but panic isn't on the list."

"But it could be," he insisted.

Kayla wanted to deny that, wanted to tell him there was no possibility of a repeat of what'd happened during their post-sex moments. However, there was a chance that the flashbacks could take over.

"I don't want to let the past dictate anything else in my life," she said instead. "I want a fresh start. I want the here and now."

She brushed her lips over his, but Cash didn't claim her mouth as he'd done seconds earlier. Instead, he stared at her with that intense gaze.

"You're saying all of this to me now because you think we're going to die," Cash grumbled.

"We might," she admitted. "And that's almost certainly playing into this. But I still want that change in my life."

She was about to add that she hoped the change would include him. But his phone buzzed again, and just like that, the heat and the moment were both lost. Kayla had no idea if or when she'd get another opportunity to finish telling him what she wanted for her future.

Because they might not have a future.

Not if Harvin had his way.

On a heavy breath, he took out his phone, and Kayla saw Ruby's name on the screen before she moved off Cash's lap and stood. He stood, too, and he took the call on speaker.

His boss didn't make them wait long to tell them why she'd called. "Harvin's on the line," Ruby said. "And he's set up a meeting place."

"Where?" Cash asked.

"He won't say. The asshole won't say," she repeated, the frustration in her voice. "For now, he wants Kayla and you to go to Coyote Creek Road. It's about twenty minutes from your place."

Cash shook his head and started a search on his phone. "I've never heard of it," he told Ruby.

"Neither had I, but here's what my techs found as soon as we had a location. The road is about ten miles long, narrow, and is in serious disrepair since there are no ranches or residences on it any longer. Lots of woods, a dried up creek, and several abandoned houses and barns."

Sweet heaven. It would be impossible for even Maverick Ops to cover that much ground.

"Hold on a sec," Ruby said. "Harvin apparently has something else to say, and he wants us to see a picture."

Kayla's heart dropped. She couldn't imagine any picture from a killer would be a good thing.

Ruby was only off the line for a couple of seconds, and when she came back on, she was muttering some raw profanity. "I'm forwarding you the photo," she blurted. "Harvin says you've got fifteen minutes to get to Coyote Creek Road, or he starts shooting."

Cash's phone dinged with the incoming photo, and he turned his phone so they could both see it when it loaded.

Kayla groaned. She'd been right about this not being good.

And it wasn't.

God, it wasn't.

———————— ★☆★ ————————

CHAPTER SEVEN

--- ★☆★ ---

Harvin had another hostage. This one in a Santa suit, too.

Even though Cash wasn't actually looking at the photo at the moment, he could still see it so damn clearly in his mind. That image meant he was having a fierce battle with himself to focus on stopping Harvin from killing not just the new hostage.

But also Kayla and him.

That fierce mental battle was involving several moving parts. Some literal ones since he was driving. While Cash did that, he listened to the chatter on his phone of Ruby barking out instructions. Ones that would hopefully give Kayla and him a decent shot at surviving this.

"I want feed from the drone as soon as it's in place," he heard Ruby tell one of the techs.

That drone would give them info to help them pinpoint Harvin's location. Once they had that, then Ruby could put some boots on the ground to get them near the site. Close enough not to be easily seen but to be able to provide backup.

Cash trusted the "boots" that Ruby had chosen. Jericho McKenna and Rafe Cross. Both veteran members of Maverick Ops, and they were already on their way to Coyote Creek Road. They would be armed and ready.

But Harvin would be ready as well.

And Cash had to consider that Harvin was nowhere near the location where Kayla, Jericho, Rafe, and he were heading. In fact, the attack could take place enroute, and that was the reason Cash was keeping watch around them.

Not an easy task.

The entire area was basically jammed with trees, thick underbrush, and bluffs. Too damn many places for Harvin to lie in wait and ambush them in a hail of gunfire.

The SUV was bullet-resistant, but that didn't mean shots couldn't get through. It also didn't mean Harvin wouldn't resort to something more powerful than bullets. He could use explosives or even strip spikes on the road to disable the tires so he could then move in for an easier kill.

In case any of that happened, Cash did have plenty of backup weapons in the vehicle, but he didn't want to get into that kind of pissing contest with some asshole who'd set up the sick rules of this deadly game.

"I'm tracking you," Ruby said, "and it appears you're within a minute of taking the turn onto Coyote Creek Road."

"I am," Cash verified. "No sign of Harvin. Any further word from him?"

"Not yet, but I suspect he's got the road under surveillance and will know when you're there," Ruby answered, and then she paused. "How are you holding up, Kayla?"

Kayla opened her mouth, no doubt to get an automatic answer of *I'm fine*, but then she stopped and perhaps did some rethinking. "I'm scared, but that won't stop me. This is probably the fastest way to prevent Harvin from killing anyone else."

Ruby made a sound that might have been agreement. Or concern that this was a huge mistake. Cash had the same worry. He was essentially taking Kayla straight into the arms of a killer.

"Harvin had rules, and, Kayla, I have one for you, too," Ruby went on a moment later. "Cash is well trained for ops like this so I want you to follow his lead."

Kayla sighed. "He'll just tell me to stay behind him. He'll put himself in immediate danger to save me."

"Yes, he will," Ruby verified before Cash could say that was the absolute truth. "And that's a good thing. Harvin wants both of you, and if you go in side by side, it'll give him an easier shot to take you both out at the same time."

Kayla stayed quiet a moment and then muttered, "All right."

"Good," Ruby said. "Glad we're of a like mind on

this. Now, I'm going to mute what's going on here so you can focus on what's happening around you. I'll be able to hear you so if you need to ask me something, just let me know, and I'll come back on the line."

The background chatter ended, and the silence settled around them. Cash wasn't sure that was better for his concentration because his thoughts assaulted him. Somehow, he had to make this work. He had to put an end to Harvin's reign of terror and keep Kayla alive.

Somehow.

Cash slowed to take the turn onto the road where the trees and shrubs were even thicker. Weeds were growing up through the surface of the cracked asphalt and along the ditches. He didn't see Harvin or any signs of weapons or surveillance equipment, but that didn't mean any or all of those weren't around.

The SUV bobbled over the surface, which was basically one deep pothole right after another. Since he was creeping along, Cash had only gone about twenty yards when Ruby came back on the line.

"Harvin's made contact," Ruby said, her voice sounding tight but focused. "There's an old, abandoned store about a quarter of a mile from where you are. Stop there in the parking lot and await instructions."

"Hell," Cash grumbled. That wouldn't give Jericho and Rafe much time to get in place. "Do we have drone images yet?"

"Just got them," Ruby confirmed, "and I'm

sending them to you now. Note the helicopter on the road just up from the store."

The feed loaded on his dash monitor, and Cash did indeed see the chopper, which would be out of sight from the store since it was on the backside of a steep curve in the road. That was no doubt how Harvin had arrived.

And how he planned to escape.

"Is Harvin actually in the store?" Cash asked.

"Possibly. Someone is anyway. The drone just checked the store for heat sources," Ruby explained, "and there are six people inside. Three more on the sides and back of the building."

Cash cursed again. "That's a lot of hired muscle. That chopper's not big enough to transport nine people."

"Agreed. There must be another vehicle parked somewhere out of sight. The drone is searching for it." Ruby stopped when there was some more chatter in the background. "Rafe and Jericho are still ten minutes out. Try to stall until they're in place."

"Will do," Cash assured her, and he hoped that would be possible.

He kept driving, kept glancing around. And he saw no one or nothing suspicious. Not until the store came into view. Like the road surface, the concrete on the parking lot had plenty of weeds, and from the looks of it, some of them had been recently trampled down.

"I don't see anyone on the sides of the building,"

Kayla relayed to Ruby. "Are they still there?"

"Yes, according to the drone feed," Ruby verified. "They're both belly down, and judging from the angle of their hands and body, they're both heavily armed."

Of course, they were. Whoever these people were, they were hired guns, and Cash only hoped they didn't have orders to kill Kayla and him on sight. If so, they'd be gunned down the moment they stepped from the SUV unless Jericho and Rafe managed to get into place first to neutralize them.

"Get down lower in the seat," Cash told Kayla as he pulled to a stop in front of the store.

Or rather in front of the building that had once been a store. There wasn't much left of the original structure. Part of the roof and some of the walls had been caved in and all the windows had been broken.

"I can't see anyone inside," Cash told Ruby. "Where were the heat sources the drone found?"

"All the way at the back of the building. My guess is it's some kind of storage area."

That made sense. Being out of sight was better protection for Harvin and the hostage. Well, it was if the building itself was secure enough. It looked ready to fall down with a gust of wind.

"How the hell did Harvin know about this place?" Cash asked, still keeping watch.

"His grandparents used to own a hunting camp near there," Ruby supplied. "He spent a lot of time in this area as a kid."

So, Harvin would know the terrain. Which gave him a huge advantage, especially with all the hired guns he'd brought with him.

"Jericho and Rafe are still six minutes out," Ruby added a moment later. "They've parked just off the main road and are on foot now."

Ruby had barely finished that update just as there was some movement in the doorway. Cash spotted the man in the bright red Santa suit, and he saw the same terror on this one's face as he had from those in the live feeds.

Cash also saw Harvin.

The SOB was behind his hostage and had a gun to the man's head. Harvin was also grinning in triumph, and Cash had to choke down the rage that shot through him.

"Come on and join us," Harvin called out. "Oh, and that's not an invitation. It's an order. Move now."

Shit. Jericho and Rafe weren't nearly close enough, and Cash was trying to figure out how to stall. But he didn't get the chance.

The sound of the gunshot blasted through the air. And the Santa yelled in pain.

"He shot him," Kayla blurted. "Harvin shot him."

Yeah, he had but not in the guy's head. Not a kill shot. Instead, Cash saw the blood spread over the shoulder of the suit.

"For every second you piss around and don't get out, I'll keep putting bullets in him," Harvin shouted. "Message received?"

"Message received," Cash spat out, and he opened his door and stepped out. "Get out on this side behind me," he whispered to Kayla.

She nodded and crawled across the console and driver's seat to get out. Thankfully, she stayed behind him.

"Oh, I can see you wore Kevlar just for me," Harvin announced in that mock sappy voice. "Well, don't just stand there. Come on in. My trigger finger's getting itchy, and I might put another shot in Santa if you drag your feet."

Cash started walking, but since Harvin hadn't ordered him to put up his hands, he kept them by his side so he could better reach the flares and the slingshot.

"All right, stop for a sec," Harvin instructed when Kayla and Cash were still about ten feet away from the doorway.

There was the sound of someone moving on the side of the building, and a man wearing all black and wearing a ski mask scurried out. He used a handheld metal detector wand on Cash. Then, on Kayla.

"She's got the knife," the thug told Harvin.

"Good. Then, she's obeyed the rules," Harvin said. "Now, go back to your post since I suspect Ruby Maverick will have some of her operatives coming along shortly. The second you spot them, shoot to kill and go for the throats or thighs. Kevlar won't do shit to protect them there."

No, it wouldn't, and that knotted every muscle in

Cash's body. But he had to hope that Jericho and Rafe would see the threat and neutralize it.

"Come on in," Harvin went off, his attention going back to Kayla and him after his thug had run back to the side of the building.

Keeping the bleeding Santa as a human shield, Harvin backed up enough so that Kayla and he could enter. They stepped in, and Cash immediately did a sweeping glance around the place.

There was debris everywhere. Old boxes, wood and shingles from the roof, and some trash. The fast food bags and the remains of a campfire let him know that the store had gotten some visitors over the years.

"That way," Harvin ordered, tipping his head to the back of the building.

As Ruby had speculated, it appeared to be a storage room. One without a door. Probably not a window either. There was no sunlight coming from there, but the area was lit up, maybe with flashlights since there was no electricity.

"Keep walking," Harvin snapped, the sickening glee still in his voice.

Kayla and he were moving at a snail's pace, as slow as Cash thought it was safe to do. He didn't want to give Harvin an excuse to shoot the hostage again, but he wanted to buy that time for Jericho and Rafe.

"Why did you want me to bring the knife?" Kayla asked.

Harvin looked at her and beamed. "Oh, you'll

soon find out, bitch. Soon," he emphasized.

Harvin stopped outside the storage room and again tipped his head for them to go inside. Cash did, fully expecting to come face to face with three more ski mask wearing gunmen.

But he didn't.

Thanks to about a half dozen large flashlights, he had no trouble seeing there was one such thug in the corner, and he was holding an assault rifle. He had it aimed at the three women kneeling on the floor.

"Fuck," Cash growled.

All three were wearing Christmas costumes. One was an elf, another an angel, and the one in the middle was dressed as Mrs. Santa. The elf and the Mrs. Santa gave him the flashbacks from hell since those were the costumes Kira and Kayla had been wearing when Virgil had attacked them.

Judging from the gasp Kayla made, she was getting a shitload of flashbacks, too. Of course, she was. All of this was meant to dick around with their heads.

And Harvin was succeeding.

Not just for Kayla and him but also for the hostages.

Cash glanced at the trio again, and he was betting not a one of them was over eighteen. Again, Harvin was trying to mimic the scene when Kira had been murdered. Each of the hostages had their hands tied in front of them and were gagged and blindfolded. Despite the blindfolds, tears had streaked down all of their cheeks, and they were clearly terrified.

"I didn't want to leave the ladies out of this adventure," Harvin boasted. "I found this group going to their high school party and brought them here to join in on the fun. Does it bring back memories?" He didn't wait for an answer. "I sure hope so. I want you reliving every last second of your sister's life."

They were, and Cash prayed it didn't lead to Kayla having a panic attack. Or a full mental breakdown.

Harvin's expression turned to ice. "Do as I say, or they get to feel bullets being fired into various parts of their bodies."

It took Cash a moment to get his jaw unclenched so he could speak to this piece of shit. "We're here, aren't we? We've done as you've said. Now, let them go and you can deal with us."

Harvin pretended to think about that and shook his head. "I think I'll hang onto them just in case your Maverick Ops' friends get past my guys out there. I'll call them insurance. FYI, they're nearly the same age you were when you caused my uncle to end up in jail."

Yeah, and that meant they were the same age as Kira had been when said asshole uncle had killed her.

Behind him, he could hear Kayla's breath start to gust, and he could practically feel the panic rising in her. "What do you want?" she snapped, surprising Cash. Her voice sounded a hell of a lot stronger than he'd expected. "Am I to use this knife on you?"

"You wish, bitch," Harvin spat out. "But I want

you to try. I want you to come at me and plunge the knife...here." He used his left hand to reach around to the front of his hostage, and he tapped the guy on the heart. "I know you're good at killing people because you killed my dad."

There was plenty of emotion in Harvin's voice now. And worse, that was an unhinged look in his eyes. That's when Cash knew that Harvin didn't intend for any of the hostages to get out of this alive.

Cash sized up the thug in the corner. His rifle was still pointed at the girls. Harvin's gun was pressed to his shield's temple. So, neither of them had taken aim at Kayla and him. That could change in a blink, of course. But maybe a blink was all he needed.

"Get down," Cash whispered to Kayla, and before the words were even out of his mouth, he yanked out one of the flares and set it off.

Immediately, intense red light began to spew through the room.

But so did the sound of gunfire.

Someone pulled the trigger.

★☆★

CHAPTER EIGHT

———— ★☆★ ————

Everything seemed to happen at once for Kayla. The sound of that gunshot, the hiss of the flare, the red smoke-like light, and the loud gasp of someone in pain.

Her heart dropped, and even as Cash was pushing her to the floor, she reached out, trying to help him. Trying to make sure he hadn't been shot.

It took her some horrifying moments to realize the sound of pain hadn't come from him but rather from the Santa hostage. Through the whirls of spewing light, Kayla saw the man fall to the ground.

Maybe dead.

But she prayed not. *God, please, no.* Enough innocent people had died because of Harvin.

Kayla caught another glimpse of someone. Of Harvin this time. And he no longer had his human shield to protect him. He scrambled forward, reaching for one of the girls, no doubt so he could use her to protect himself, but Cash lunged at him to stop him.

Cash slammed into Harvin, both of them flying

across the room and landing with loud, jarring thuds on the floor. The girls were all sobbing now, their voices muffled but still audible behind the gags. The sounds they were making blended with those of the fight.

And the running footsteps.

Again, it took another couple of seconds for Kayla to figure out what was happening, and what was happening was very bad. The thug with the assault rifle was charging right toward her.

He was coming to grab her, maybe to kill her, maybe to use her as leverage to get Cash off his boss.

Kayla didn't intend for him to get the chance to do any of those things. She didn't think, and she damn sure didn't panic. She stood, keeping the knife by the side of her leg. Waiting for the bastard.

And he came all right.

He bolted around the girls and toward her, and through the slits of the ski mask, she could see the cold, hard glare he was aiming at her. Kayla aimed something of her own at him. Not a glare.

But the knife.

She wouldn't be able to go for his neck the way she had with Alvin because the thug might see it and knock it from her hand. Instead, she waited, and the moment the asshole reached out for her, she maneuvered the knife, aiming for his groin and thigh, hoping to hit the femoral artery.

Kayla rammed the blade into him as hard as she could.

And she didn't miss.

She stabbed him three times, until the blood started to spurt across her and the room. The man didn't make it even another inch before he tumbled face first into a heap right at her feet. If he wasn't already dead, he sure as heck soon would be, and Kayla felt nothing but relief about that. He wouldn't be able to hurt the girls or her, and he wouldn't be able to help his boss.

In case the hired thug had one last ditch effort in him, Kayla picked up his assault rifle and threw it across the room. She didn't even consider trying to use it since she'd never fired a gun like that. Instead, she lifted the knife again and turned to try to help Cash.

Another sound stopped her.

More gunshots.

They were coming from outside, but one ripped through the wall and landed heaven knew where.

Kayla felt her heart start pounding. Her head, too. And her breath seemed to vanish. She knew these signs. They were the start of a panic attack, and it would have been so easy just to give in to it.

She didn't.

Instead, she whirled around and pinned her attention on Cash. He was in a fight for his life with Harvin, a man who outsized him by a good fifty pounds. Worse though, Harvin still had his gun.

And he pulled the damn trigger.

The shot was deafening, echoing off the walls,

and for way too many heart stopping moments, Kayla thought that Cash had been hit. It crushed everything inside to consider that he might be dead.

Yelling at the top of her lungs, she shoved aside the panic and charged at Harvin, ready to use the knife on him. Ready to send the son of a bitch straight to hell where he belonged.

She reached the men, already bringing up the knife, but with the tangle of Cash's and Harvin's bodies, she couldn't tell where to stab. She certainly didn't want to risk hitting Cash.

With the flare lights clearing, she saw Harvin bashed his gun against the side of Cash's head. The SOB didn't stop there. He shifted the gun, trying to take aim at Cash. Kayla shifted, too, trying to get into position to either stab Harvin or grab that gun.

"It's Rafe and me," someone called out. Jericho, probably. And they were running toward the storage room. "We've taken care of the assholes outside."

Good. That meant they couldn't come in and try to finish what their boss had started.

Kayla stayed put, still watching for an opening in the fight where she could help, but from the corner of her eye she saw Jericho and Rafe come rushing in. They wouldn't have a clean shot either. They wouldn't be able to stop Harvin from trying to kill Cash.

That thought had barely crossed her mind when there was another gunshot.

And it'd come from Harvin's gun.

She yelled again and was about to launch herself at Harvin. But it was already too late. Blood was spurting everywhere, and she couldn't tell if it was coming from Cash or Harvin.

Then, she saw it.

The arrowhead rock that Cash had had in his pocket. It was now in Harvin's neck.

And Harvin was very much dead.

The relief flooded through her, causing her legs to buckle. Kayla dropped to her knees, and she latched onto Cash to pull him into her arms.

★☆★

CHAPTER NINE

———— ★☆★ ————

Cash lay curled up on the sofa with Kayla and stared at the twinkling lights of the Christmas tree. The *fully decorated* tree that Kayla and he had done shortly after they'd arrived back from their hellish ordeal with Harvin.

At first, it had seemed like a strange thing for Kayla to want to do, but she had requested it right after they'd showered, washing away the blood that'd gotten on them during the attack. Cash had been pleased to hear her ask for such a thing since he'd been bracing himself for her to deal with the flood of emotions that had to be going through her.

But the flood had stayed quiet.

And together, they'd decorated every single inch of the tree.

Then, they'd both given into the adrenaline crashes from hell and had cuddled up on the sofa. Kayla had fallen asleep, again something he hadn't expected, but he was damn glad she had. He only hoped that she was having peaceful dreams and not the shitty nightmares that Harvin and his kin had given her.

Cash figured some nightmares were going to be inevitable, but there were some big-assed bright spots, too. The last Santa hostage was alive. Yeah, he was in ICU and would likely need lots of rehab and PT, but the signs were good that he would eventually recover.

There was a bright spot for the three teenage girls, too. They were all safe and sound back home, where they'd be having Christmas with their families. It was truly a miracle that they'd all three come out of the ordeal with only minor physical injuries. Just some cuts and bruises. Of course, like the Santa hostage, it would no doubt take them a while and some therapy to deal with the mental stuff. Harvin had left them with a shitload of memories that could follow them forever.

Still, they were alive, and Harvin wasn't.

Harvin's four hired thugs were dead, too, thanks to the three that Jericho and Rafe had shot outside the store. Kayla had taken care of the fourth one, and whether it had occurred to her or not, once again she'd saved herself.

Cash hoped that gave her strength to get through the next couple of days.

As if she'd sensed he was thinking about her, Kayla stirred, and her eyes opened. She was smiling —something he was damn glad to see—and her smile got even wider when she looked at him.

"It's not a dream," she muttered.

"What do you mean?" he had to ask.

"You. This." She fluttered her hand toward the tree. "Us. We're alive, and we have a Christmas tree."

There was so much enthusiasm in her voice. Actually, there was downright joy in that tone and expression. Her face was bright and happy, and he forced himself not to think of the bandage on her head from Alvin's attack. In fact, he forced himself to focus only on her.

Not a hard task.

Kayla was her usual stunning self. She might have argued with him about that assessment since she had on no makeup, and her hair had dried at some odd angles since she'd fallen asleep while it was still damp.

"It's Christmas," she murmured, and again, there was that joy.

And it was infectious since Cash was starting to feel it as well. In fact, he was starting to feel a lot of things, some that he probably shouldn't, but it was hard for his thoughts not to turn dirty with Kayla pressed against him like this.

It was more than the body to body contact, though. It was the way she was looking at him. Straight in the eyes, and she wasn't trying to inch away. There wasn't a trace of panic in sight so, Cash tested the waters, ready to pull back if necessary.

He brushed his mouth over hers. "Merry Christmas," he murmured.

Cash might have eased back to gauge her reaction,

but Kayla slid her hand around the back of his neck and pulled him to her for another kiss. It was long, slow, and incredibly hot.

Kayla seemed to pour a whole lot of emotions into that kiss. Maybe because she had no choice about that, not with the old heat between them generating some new fires. It was the same for him. Cash put some emotion into it, taking a risk and hoping that the risk paid off.

It did.

Kayla made a silky sound of pleasure and just kept her mouth on his. Since that was a really good sign, Cash ran his tongue over her bottom lip and went French with the kiss. His reward was another of Kayla's moans and more flames to that growing fire.

Kayla moved, turning so her body was fully pressed against his. And his dick certainly appreciated that. Still, Cash tried to keep himself in check since he knew Kayla could put an end to this in a blink.

But she didn't.

She kept up the kissing and added some touching, too. She slid her hand down his chest. Then under his shirt. Her fingers played with the muscles on his stomach. And his chest. She lit fires along the way.

And need.

Plenty of need.

Again, Cash tried to rein things in, but Kayla didn't make that easy. He got a flash of memories. Not of the attacks. But of their intense making-out sessions when they'd been teenagers. Those sessions had been sweet torture with a whole lot of pleasure.

But not full sex.

That hadn't happened until they were adults, but before that, there had been times like this. So many kisses. So many touches. And, yeah, more than an orgasm or two from what turned out to be hand jobs. Cash was considering going for that now, but Kayla took matters into her own hand.

Literally.

She ran her palm past the waist of his cargo pants and into his boxers.

Cash cursed and jolted but in a good way at her touch. The pleasure fired through him, and he instantly wanted more. He wanted to give more, too, so he shifted enough so that he could slip his hand under her top. Since she wasn't wearing a bra, he was able to slide his fingers over her nipples.

Kayla gasped, and it was a familiar sound. All pleasure. So, Cash gave her more. He shoved up her top and replaced his fingers with her mouth.

It was the right move.

She cursed him but in a good, dirty way, and while he tasted every inch of her breasts, she got her hands on his hard-on. Familiar territory for her, and she obviously remembered the *terrain*. She gripped and touched, sliding her thumb over the tip of his erection.

Cash didn't have the breath to curse her, and the heat was growing by leaps and bounds. So was the urgency building inside him so he did a turnabout fair play move. He moved his hand into her shorts and found exactly what he was looking for.

She bucked against his fingers and began fighting to get off her clothes. Those clothes were the enemy now, and she clearly wanted to be naked.

He helped with that.

Mindful of her stitches, Cash eased off the shirt. Then, the boxers she was wearing.

"I want you naked now," she insisted, yanking off his shirt and going after his zipper. "And you'd better have a condom."

"In my wallet," he managed to say.

Kayla took that as a personal challenge, to get the condom and take off his pants at the same time. Since the need was pushing hard for this to happen now, Cash helped with that. He got the condom, tossing his wallet to the floor, and then seconds later, his pants and boxers ended up there as well.

Despite that urgency, Cash studied Kayla's face while he got on the condom. At least that's what he tried to do, but she began a frantic flurry of kissing and touching. The woman was clearly on a mission for this to turn into full-blown sex.

And Cash was more than willing to make that happen.

He shifted again, moving her on top of him so she could stop if the panic came. But there was no panic in her expression or in her moves. She took him inside her and rode him hard and fast. Just as the heat and need were dictating.

She anchored her hands on his chest, lowering her head to kiss him while she thrust onto him. Over and over. Faster. Then, even faster. Until Cash felt the need clawing its way to the finish.

Kayla did some finishing.

He felt the climax ripple through her, saw the glow of pure pleasure on her face, and that was all Cash needed. He let go, letting his own climax consume him as he pulled Kayla into his arms.

———— ★☆★ ————

CHAPTER TEN

———— ★☆★ ————

Kayla woke from her nap to two amazing things. A Christmas tree and a naked Cash with her on the sofa, a spot they'd returned to shortly after they'd taken a post-sex shower together.

Where they'd had more sex.

Both times Cash had no doubt been worried about her having a panic attack, but it hadn't come. Just the opposite. Both the before and after part of the sex had been pure pleasure.

And she was looking forward to more of that pleasure.

She stared up at him, not surprised to see that he was wide awake. She'd spent most of the day napping, recovering from the adrenaline crash, but he seemed to need no such downtime.

However, he might need thinking time. Some hours, or days, alone to try to sort everything that'd happened in the past thirty-six or so hours. That's why Kayla had decided to hold off on telling him how she felt about him.

"I always thought you were my soulmate," he

blurted, and she wasn't sure who was more surprised by that, him or her.

Surprised, but in her case, very pleased. It was a nice sensation to go along with her sated body.

"Soulmate, huh?" she repeated.

He cursed and generally looked miserable about his confession. "You don't have to say or do anything —"

"I like the sound of that. Soulmate," she said again, smiling around the word. "It's sort of like Christmas."

Cash lifted his eyebrow, beckoning for her to explain.

"Two happy words," she tried. "Both filled with... stuff," Kayla settled for saying. "Good stuff," she amended. "Happiness, joy, and love stuff."

The surprise came again, both to Cash and her, and she knew exactly what had put that shock in his eyes.

The l-word.

He probably hadn't been ready to hear that, but she decided to finish what she'd started.

"When we were in the fight for our lives, there was one thought that kept going through my head," she explained. "Well, two thoughts actually. One was I didn't want to lose you, and the other was that I'm in love with you. I have been since I was eight, and you spent your last dollar, literally, to buy me a replacement ice cream cone."

The corner of his mouth lifted into a near smile.

"That's when you fell in love with me?"

She nodded and because she couldn't help herself, Kayla kissed him. The heat and pleasure began to stir again.

He eased back from her so they were eye to eye and breath to breath. "I fell in love with you before that," he said.

Kayla thought that might be BS, but then that wasn't a BS kind of look in his eyes.

"Soulmate," he repeated, and Cash snapped his fingers. "It happened the first time I saw you, and it's never stopped. Never," he emphasized.

Kayla felt a new sensation blending with the pleasure and heat. She felt the love and realized it had always been there. Right from the start.

"So, what do soulmates do on Christmas?" she asked, nipping his bottom lip with her teeth.

Cash nipped her lip right back. "They kiss, make love and say a lot of I love you's. It's the perfect gift," he added.

Yes, it was. The soulmate trifecta. And Kayla decided to get started with another round of that gift giving. She latched onto Cash and pulled him to her for a long Christmas kiss.

★☆★

ABOUT THE HARD JUSTICE TEXAS SERIES:

★☆★

The Maverick Ops team members are former military and cops who assist law enforcement in cold cases and hot investigations where lives are on the line. Their specialty is rescuing kidnapped victims, tracking down killers and protecting those in the path of danger. Maverick Ops is known for doing what it does best-- delivering some hard justice.

★☆★

ABOUT THE AUTHOR:

———— ★☆★ ————

Former Air Force Captain Delores Fossen is a New York Times, USA Today, Amazon and Publisher's Weekly bestselling author whose books have sold over nine million copies. She's received the Booksellers Best Award for Best Romantic Suspense and the Romantic Times Reviewers Choice Award. In addition, she's had nearly a hundred short stories and articles published in national magazines. You can contact the author through her webpage.

———— ★☆★ ————

HARD JUSTICE, TEXAS SERIES BOOKS BY DELORES FOSSEN:

Lone Star Rescue (book 1)

Lone Star Showdown (book 2)

Lone Star Payback (book 3)

Lone Star Protector (book 4)

Lone Star Witness (book 5)

Lone Star Target (book 6)

Lone Star Secrets (book 7)

Lone Star Hostage (book 8)

Lone Star Redemption (book 9)

Lone Star Christmas Mission (novella)

———————— ★☆★ ————————

Visit deloresfossen.com for more titles and release dates. Also sign up for Delores' newsletter at https://www.deloresfossen.com/contactnewsletter.html

———————— ★☆★ ————————

OTHER BOOKS BY DELORES FOSSEN:

Appaloosa Pass Ranch

1 - Lone Wolf Lawman (Nov-2015)

2 - Taking Aim at the Sheriff (Dec-2015)

3 - Trouble with a Badge (Apr-2016)

4 - The Marshal's Justice (May-2016)

5 - Six-Gun Showdown (Aug-2016)

6 - Laying Down the Law (Sep-2016)

Blue River Ranch

1 - Always a Lawman (Dec-2017)

2 - Gunfire on the Ranch (Jan-2018)

3 - Lawman From Her Past (Mar-2018)

4 - Roughshod Justice (Apr-2018)

Coldwater, Texas
1 - Lone Star Christmas (Sep-2018)
1.5 - Lone Star Midnight (Jan-2019)
2 - Hot Texas Sunrise (Mar-2019)
2.5 - Texas at Dusk (Jun-2019)
3 - Sweet Summer Sunset (Jun-2019)
4 - A Coldwater Christmas (Sep-2019)

Cowboy Brothers in Arms
1 - Heart Like a Cowboy (Dec-2023)
2 - Always a Maverick (May-2024)
3 – Cowboying Up (working title) 2024

Five Alarm Babies
1 - Undercover Daddy (May-2007)
2 - Stork Alert // Whose Baby? (Aug-2007)
3 - The Christmas Clue (Nov-2007)
4 - Newborn Conspiracy (Feb-2008)
5 - The Horseman's Son // The Cowboy's Son (Mar-2008)

Last Ride, Texas

LONE STAR CHRISTMAS MISSION

1 - Spring at Saddle Run (May-2021)

2 - Christmas at Colts Creek (Nov-2021)

3 - Summer at Stallion Ridge (Apr-2022)

3.5 - Second Chance at Silver Springs (Oct-2022)

4 - Mornings at River's End Ranch (Dec-2022)

4.5 - Breaking Rules at Nightfall Ranch (Feb-2023)

5 - A Texas Kind of Cowboy (Mar-2023)

6 - Twilight at Wild Springs (Jul-2023)

The Law in Lubbock County

1 - Sheriff in the Saddle (Jul-2022)

2 - Maverick Justice (Aug-2022)

3 - Lawman to the Core (Jan-2023)

4 - Spurred to Justice (Jan-2023)

The Lawmen of Silver Creek Ranch

1 - Grayson (Nov-2011)

2 - Dade (Dec-2011)

3 - Nate (Jan-2012)

4 - Kade (Jul-2012)

5 - Gage (Aug-2012)

6 - Mason (Sep-2012)

7 - Josh (Apr-2014)

8 - Sawyer (May-2014)

9 - Landon (Nov-2016)

10 - Holden (Mar-2017)

11 - Drury (Apr-2017)

12 - Lucas (May-2017)

The Lawmen of McCall Canyon

1 - Cowboy Above the Law (Aug-2018)

2 - Finger on the Trigger (Sep-2018)

3 - Lawman with a Cause (Jan-2019)

4 - Under The Cowboy's Protection (Feb-2019)

Lone Star Ridge

1 - Tangled Up in Texas (Feb-2020)

1.5 - That Night in Texas (May-2020)

2 - Chasing Trouble in Texas (Jun-2020)

2.5 - Hot Summer in Texas (Sep-2020)

3 - Wild Nights in Texas (Oct-2020)

3.5 - Whatever Happens in Texas (Jan-2021)

4 - Tempting in Texas (Feb-2021)

5 - Corralled in Texas (Mar-2022)

Longview Ridge Ranch
1 - Safety Breach (Dec-2019)
2 - A Threat to His Family (Jan-2020)
3 - Settling an Old Score (Aug-2020)
4 - His Brand of Justice (Sep-2020)

The Marshals of Maverick County
1 - The Marshal's Hostage (May-2013)
2 - One Night Standoff (Jun-2013)
3 - Outlaw Lawman (Jul-2013)
4 - Renegade Guardian (Nov-2013)
5 - Justice Is Coming (Dec-2013)
6 - Wanted (Jan-2014)

McCord Brothers
0.5 - What Happens on the Ranch (Jan-2016)
1 - Texas on My Mind (Feb-2016)
1.5 - Cowboy Trouble (May-2016)
2 - Lone Star Nights (Jun-2016)
2.5 - Cowboy Underneath It All (Aug-2016)
3 - Blame It on the Cowboy (Oct-2016)

Mercy Ridge Lawmen

1 - Her Child to Protect (May-2021)

2 - Safeguarding the Surrogate (Jul-2021)

3 - Targeting the Deputy (Dec-2021)

4 - Pursued by the Sheriff (Jan-2022)

Mustang Ridge

1 - Christmas Rescue at Mustang Ridge (Dec-2012)

2 - Standoff at Mustang Ridge (Jan-2013)

Silver Creek Lawmen: Second Generation

1 - Targeted in Silver Creek (Jul-2023)

2 - Maverick Detective Dad (Aug-2023)

3 - Last Seen in Silver Creek (Sep-2023)

4 - Marked For Revenge (Oct-2023)

Sweetwater Ranch

1 - Maverick Sheriff (Sep-2014)

2 - Cowboy Behind the Badge (Oct-2014)

3 - Rustling Up Trouble (Nov-2014)

4 - Kidnapping in Kendall County (Dec-2014)

5 - The Deputy's Redemption (Mar-2015)

6 - Reining in Justice (Apr-2015)

7 - Surrendering to the Sheriff (Jul-2015)

8 - A Lawman's Justice (Aug-2015)

Texas Maternity Hostages

1 - The Baby's Guardian (May-2010)

2 - Daddy Devastating (Jun-2010)

3 - The Mommy Mystery (Jul-2010)

Texas Maternity: Labor and Delivery

1 - Savior in the Saddle (Nov-2010)

2 - Wild Stallion (Dec-2010)

3 - The Texas Lawman's Last Stand (Jan-2011)

Texas Paternity

1 - Security Blanket (Oct-2008)

2 - Branded By The Sheriff (Jan-2009)

3 - Expecting Trouble (Feb-2009)

4 - Secret Delivery (Mar-2009)

5 - Christmas Guardian (Oct-2009)

A Wrangler's Creek Novel
1 - Those Texas Nights (Jan-2017)
2 - No Getting Over a Cowboy (Apr-2017)
3 - Branded as Trouble (Jul-2017)
4 - Lone Star Cowboy (Nov-2016)
5 - One Good Cowboy (Feb-2017)
6 - Just Like a Cowboy (May-2017)
7 - Texas-Sized Trouble (Jan-2018)
8 - Lone Star Blues (Apr-2018)
9 - The Last Rodeo (Jul-2018)
10 - Cowboy Dreaming (Dec-2017)
11 - Cowboy Heartbreaker (Mar-2018)
12 - Cowboy Blues (May-2018)

Daddy Corps
G.I. Cowboy (Apr-2011)

Ice Lake
Cold Heat (Jan-2012)

Kenner County Crime Unit
She's Positive (Jul-2009)

Men on a Mission
Marching Orders (Mar-2003)

Shivers
20 - His to Possess (Oct-2014)

The Silver Star of Texas
Trace Evidence In Tarrant County // For Justice and Love (Feb-2007)
Questioning The Heiress (Jul-2008)
Shotgun Sheriff (Feb-2010)

Top Secret Babies
Mommy Under Cover (Feb-2005)

EXCERPT

OUTLAW RIDGE: HAYES

Book 1, Outlaw Ridge: Hard Justice Series

Chapter One

Hayes Brodie was so not in the mood for this shitshow. Then again, he was never in the mood to deal with a tanked-up asshole who'd just tried to kill him.

Shortly after said attempted murder, Hayes had managed to restrain the asshole—AKA Petey McGrath. He'd done that by putting him in a headlock and then slapping plastic cuffs on both his hands and his ankles.

That hadn't stopped Petey though.

Nope.

Despite not having full use of his hands or feet, Petey had still tried to punch and kick Hayes. And, of course, the restraints hadn't stopped the idiot either from spewing a string of uncreative, f-word-laced profanity.

That cursing had continued nonstop as Hayes had loaded him into his SUV and belted him into the backseat so they could begin the ten-minute drive to the Outlaw Ridge Sheriff's Office.

Hayes had a mountain of gratitude that he hadn't had to drive Petey all the way into San Antonio, a good hour away. It was late, going on midnight, and he was over and done dealing with this clown. He could stash him in the Outlaw Ridge jail and have someone from San Antonio PD come and collect him. Then, Hayes' mission would be done, and Petey would become someone else's problem.

With Petey still cursing a blue streak and doing his best to inflict harm to anyone or anything in his limited reach, Hayes turned into the parking lot of the sheriff's office. There was a cruiser and a red truck in the reserved spaces, so he figured there'd be at least one unlucky deputy on duty. Unlucky because he or she would soon get a dose of Petey.

Hayes pulled to a stop in the visitor's space behind the cruiser just as another vehicle, a Jeep, turned into the parking lot. He instantly went on alert. Petey had almost certainly pissed off a whole bunch of the wrong people with his antics, and Hayes thought this might be one of them coming to settle a score.

But that wasn't the case.

He sighed though when the tall woman with the short, choppy brown hair stepped from the Jeep. She was wearing a dark blue Outlaw Ridge PD uniform.

Deputy Jemma Salvetti.

Someone he did his best to avoid. Even when

certain parts of his body, especially the brainless part of him in his boxers, wanted no such avoiding. They'd been on a "blind" date, a setup at one of those stupid escape room deals where he'd first interacted with Jemma and felt the stirrings of heat.

Stirrings that he'd immediately shut down.

Or rather, Hayes had tried to do that anyway.

But no matter what the brainless part of him wanted, Jemma was hands-off for a whole lot of damn good reasons. Too bad those damn good reasons hadn't stopped his so-called friends from making sure Jemma was at any and all social events that Hayes attended.

"Hayes?" Jemma greeted, and, yeah, it was a question.

Even though he lived just a few miles outside of the small ranching town of Outlaw Ridge, and there were those matchmaking attempts, he didn't make it to the sheriff's office that often. That was in part because of his wanting to avoid Jemma but mainly since he didn't have a lot of business with them.

As an operative for the elite private security company Strike Force, he had missions all over the country. Missions involving rescues, hostage situations, missing persons, and other assorted felonious activities. But in his seven and a half years of working for Strike Force, this was a first for him to have apprehended a fugitive so close to Outlaw Ridge.

"Jemma," he greeted back.

In hindsight, he should have realized that she could be on duty. After all, despite being in her early thirties, she was pretty much a rookie. She'd had less than a year on the force after giving up her lucrative and successful law practice. Rookies usually got stuck on the night shift.

"What brings you here?" she asked. Even though she had that rookie label, it was an all-cop glance that she made to his backseat, where Petey was now thrashing his shoulder against the window.

"That's Petey McGrath," he said, tipping his head to the guy. "He assaulted his eighty-two-year-old grandmother, robbed her, and fled with money that he probably needed to pay off some loan sharks. His eighty-three-year-old grandfather took extreme objection to that and asked Strike Force to work with SAPD to track him down fast. I was lucky enough to locate him first, and I was hoping the sheriff's office could hold him until morning."

Jemma eyed Petey, sighed, and nodded. "What was he doing in Outlaw Ridge?"

"His grandparents have a fishing cabin about five miles away, and Petey set off a silent security alarm when he broke in. The granddad called to let me know that, so I drove straight to the cabin and found him."

"The sonofabitch punched me in the stomach," Petey complained.

Hayes huffed. "Only after he tried to stab me with a kitchen knife. I knocked that out of his hand, and he tried to kick me in the balls and pull my hair. Before he resorted to biting or some other insulting attack generally reserved for eight-year-old kids, I punched him in the gut to knock the wind out of him and then restrained him."

"You sonofabitch," Petey repeated.

Hayes had been called much worse, but as former Delta Force special ops, he'd never pulled the enemy's hair. Hard not to feel anything but contempt and loathing for someone who'd fight like that.

"Are you okay?" Jemma asked, and it took Hayes a moment to realize that the question was meant for him.

"Fine," he said.

"I'm not fine," Petey howled. "I wanta file a complaint. I wanta talk to both your bosses."

Jemma rolled her eyes. "That's a lot of demands and whining for someone who assaulted a granny. Is his grandmother all right?" she tacked onto that.

"Not especially. She's in the hospital with a broken

cheekbone and two cracked ribs," Hayes explained.

Jemma's mouth tightened. Her amber eyes narrowed. And she cursed Petey under her breath. That, and the strong urge to beat the crap out of Petey, had been Hayes's reaction as well.

Jemma gave Petey a look of undiluted disgust, and she was good at it, too. Then she tipped her head toward the police station. "I'm just about to start my shift. Let's get him inside so I can do the paperwork to process him in."

Hayes hadn't exactly been holding his breath, but it had occurred to him that the small sheriff's office might not have an available cell to hold someone.

"Thanks," Hayes muttered, and he went to his SUV door to open it.

The moment Hayes unclicked the seatbelt, Petey immediately barreled out toward him. Or rather, the asshole tried to do that anyway. Hayes just stepped back and let the idiot trip on his own bound feet and tumble out of the SUV. Hayes did catch him, right before Petey would have face-planted on the pavement.

Petey didn't show any appreciation for that.

He tried to slam his elbow into Hayes' chest, but Hayes was able to dodge that. Jemma wasn't. She had stepped up to help him, and her right breast caught the impact of Petey's assault.

Hayes cursed. Jemma did, too, and she made a sharp gasp of pain, but she didn't back away. She grabbed Petey by the back of his collar, and with Hayes' muscle behind the idiot, they began to perpwalk Petey toward the station.

They stopped though when there was a squeal of brakes out on Main Street.

A black truck screeched to a stop. It was the only vehicle on the road, so at first Hayes thought it was just a lookie-loo who wanted to know what was going on.

But no.

The driver's side window came down, and thanks

to the streetlight, he caught sight of something that he sure as hell didn't want to see.

The barrel of an assault rifle.

"Get down," Hayes managed to say, and he shoved Petey to the ground. In the same motion, he took hold of Jemma's arm, hauling her down at well.

And the bullets came flying.

A spray of gunfire peppered across the parking lot, slamming into the ground and Hayes' SUV. Keeping hold of both Petey and Jemma, Hayes scrambled back, using his vehicle for cover. It was bullet resistant, but if the shooter got out of that truck, Jemma, Petey, and he would still be easy targets.

Hayes did something to prevent that.

He drew his Glock, one of the three guns he carried, and he scrambled to his feet, moving to the front end of the SUV so he could try to return fire. He cursed though when he realized he didn't have a clean shot at their attacker. There were shops and buildings on the other side of the truck, and if someone was in one of them, he could hit them with friendly fire.

Jemma went to his side, shoulder to shoulder with him, and she was about to peer out where she might have gotten her head shot off, so Hayes used his elbow to shove her back. Apparently, she didn't approve of that because she muttered some profanity.

"I'm going to shoot at the tires to hopefully get the gunman to stop firing," Hayes let her know, and he glanced at the police station. Any deputy inside would have almost certainly heard the shots and would be responding soon, and the shooter might just gun them down the moment they stepped outside.

Hayes rolled out from the SUV, came up and fired at the tires. He hit one, and while the plan worked to get the gunman to stop shooting, it was a little too effective. The driver not only stopped firing, he slammed on the accelerator and sped away.

Normally, that would have pissed Hayes off, and he would have gone after the asshole, but he looked back at Petey, who had somehow managed to get to his feet and was trying to waddle-run away.

"Damn it," Hayes muttered.

Hayes shifted directions and tackled Petey. While he was restraining this pain in his ass, again, Jemma took out her phone, and he realized she was calling dispatch so an APB could be put out on the truck.

"Dispatch isn't answering," she muttered after a couple of seconds. Frowning, she glanced in the direction where the truck had fled. "Let me get the prisoner inside, and I'll go after it. You think the shooter was gunning for Petey?"

Hayes considered that a moment. "Maybe. Obviously, he's a class A dirtbag and no doubt has plenty of enemies."

But that suddenly didn't feel right.

And Hayes didn't like that tightness that began to form in his gut. That tightness had a way of letting him know that something more than just the obvious was wrong here, and since that sensation had saved his hide a time or two, he didn't ignore it.

Still keeping watch in case the shooter returned, Jemma took hold of one of Petey's arms, and Hayes took the other. This time, it was a perp-run, and despite the man's hampered movements, he was clearly ready to get inside and away from anyone who possibly wanted him dead.

Jemma threw open the door to the police station and muttered more profanity when she stepped into a spray of water. The overhead sprinkler system was spewing, and Hayes quickly realized why. There was smoke coming from the back of the building.

"What the heck," Jemma muttered. "Trace? Clayton?" she called out, the urgency in her tone and on all over her face.

Those were no doubt the names of the deputies who were supposed to be on duty. But no one was at any of the desks in the bullpen that was in the center of the large open space.

"Trace?" Jemma tried again, and this time there was even more alarm in her voice.

No answer.

With the water continuing to shower them, Jemma let go of her grip on Petey, and taking out her phone again, she called the fire department while hurrying past the sheriff's office. Hayes kept Petey in tow and was right behind her, but he could see that it, too, was empty.

That knot in his stomach got a whole lot tighter.

She raced to the back of the building toward the source of that smoke. "Clayton?" she tried again, making another call, and he saw that she pressed Sheriff Marty Bonetti's number.

It rang. And rang and rang. Before it went to voicemail.

Jemma's breath was gusting now, but she kept searching. Kept calling out the names of the two deputies. Kept getting no response from them.

She threw open a door at the end of a narrow hall, and she switched on a light to what appeared to be a breakroom with a counter, microwave, and leather sofa well past its prime. There were some traces of smoke here coming from a trash can in the center of the room, and the water from the sprinklers had pooled on the floor.

But it wasn't just water.

There were red streaks snaking through it.

Hayes followed the source of those streaks to the far left corner of the room. And he saw them.

Two men in deputy uniforms identical to the one Jemma was wearing. The pair were on the floor, both lying in a pool of blood.

And both men were very much dead.

---------☆---------

Made in the USA
Coppell, TX
03 January 2025